PRAISE FOR RAFAEL C. CASTILLO

Castillo has the talent and background to deliver these auspicious or superstitious stories of ordinary people: frustrated husbands, disenchanted wives, sons estranged from their fathers, and unrequited love. In one story, a high school student realizes an important lesson after his grandfather dies in "House of the Dead." Two teen skateboarders vacationing in Paris take an unexpected side "trip". *Cholo* gangbangers struggle to maintain territorial control of their barrios. Crisp, witty, smart. Castillo pens it all.

—Fernando Esteban Flores, author of *Ragged Borders, Red Accordion Blues*, and *BloodSongs*. He is the Poetry Editor of *CTN: Catch the Next Journal* (New Haven, CT)

The first thing you notice in this collection of stories is the precision of language, the ability to convey complex thoughts with lyrical simplicity. In the title story, Castillo explores myth and mysticism, melding past and present with luminous wisdom. He contrasts the old with the new, a gentle blending in some stories, a harsh collision in others, but family histories are always ongoing in these tales, the past illuminating the present. Castillo is a master.

—Robert Selzer, award-winning author of *Amado Muro and Me: A tale of Honesty and Deception* and *Thursday Night at the Mall: Movies, Books, Music & Asperger's syndrome.*

Castillo is masterly at creating indelible, painterly images. Tender and moving, *The Language of Sparrows* is about people trapped in Kafkaesque dreams yet firmly planted in *terra nostra*, in the margins of society and sanity.

—B. J. Urdiales, author of *Hereafter*.

THE LANGUAGE OF SPARROWS

STORIES

RAFAEL C. CASTILLO

If there's a book that you want to read, but it hasn't been written yet, then you must write it.

— TONI MORRISON

THE LANGUAGE OF SPARROWS
AND OTHER STORIES

INTRODUCTION

JULIAN S. GARCIA

The short story genre holds great importance in American literature, originating from the rise of tabloid newspapers and periodicals in the 19th century. These publications satisfied readers' craving for engaging stories, featuring works by key American authors whose stories shaped the genre's path. Horatio Alger's uplifting rags-to-riches stories reflected the promise of the American Dream. Meanwhile, Edgar Allan Poe's skillful gothic tales established a uniquely American voice in the genres of horror and psychological fiction. William Sydney Porter, writing as O. Henry, created stories about American adventurers and detailed the lives of those seeking fortune in the growing Southwest. Together, these writers served an American audience eager for stories packed with adventure, mystery, and the unique spirit of a young nation, expressed through storytelling.

The short story gained significant popularity during the first half of the 19th century, when writers like Stephen Crane and Ambrose Bierce serialized their stories in daily newspapers. Crane's *The Red Badge of Courage*, although a novella, originally appeared as serialized segments, while Bierce's "An Occurrence at Owl Creek Bridge" demonstrated the power of the genre to convey psychological depth within a compact narrative. The demand for stories was skyrocketing, fueling a publishing boom that offered the American public stories across all genres: westerns, mysteries, horror, and romance.

Although the short story traditionally demands narrative closure, many innovative writers have experimented with open endings, intentionally leaving conflicts unresolved to reflect the inherent ambiguity of the human experience. O. Henry became especially famous for his surprise-ending stories set in the Southwest. However, his work often featured contrived conclusions that sometimes leaned toward caricature and reinforced regional stereotypes instead of challenging them.

The American Southwest became especially fertile ground for storytelling, shaped by complex historical and cultural forces. In Texas, Tejanos—the original inhabitants and landowners of Tejas—saw their world change when American immigrants, led by figures like Stephen F. Austin, declared Texas independent from Mexico. This move came in response to Mexico's ban on slavery and efforts to control immigration, leading Texas to join the United States as a slave state. The ongoing political upheaval and revolutionary activity in Mexico created a landscape full of narrative possibilities, where cultures clashed and new identities formed from the friction, even blending Spanish with English.

Within what American folklorist Americo Paredes called "Greater Mexico"—the Mexican territory influenced by American territorial expansion—a rich literary tradition took shape. Writers such as Juan Rulfo, whose sparse and haunting prose captured rural Mexican life; Jovita González, who documented the folklore and traditions of South Texas; and Mariano Azuela, author of *The Underdogs*, recorded the effects of the Mexican Revolution on everyday people. María Francisca Moya Luna, writing under the pen name Nellie Campobello, told powerful stories about the Revolution's human toll, particularly from a woman's perspective.

By the late 1960s, a significant shift in storytelling had occurred as educated Tejanos became increasingly aware of their role in shaping Texas history and culture. This heightened awareness aligned with the larger Chicano movement, motivating many to write not only as an art form but also as a way of political protest. Newspapers and journals proliferated within Chicano communities, sprouting as frequently as bluebonnets. Publications like *El Grito*, *Caracol*, *Chicano Times*, and the international *ViAztlan*, along with independent presses such as M&A Editions, Justa Editorial Press, and other indie publishers, emerged to support nascent writers. They created cuentos, poems, plays, and novels reflecting their real-life experiences.

Their voices challenged cultural stereotypes and transformed what might have been simple ideological messages into full stories about people in transition, expressing the struggle of navigating the American mainstream while maintaining their cultural roots. Achieving this required advanced storytelling skills, including nuanced dialogue and inventive narrative structures that could reveal complex cultural and psychological truths.

One of those writers who responded to the call with notable success was Rafael C. Castillo. My collaborative friendship with him spans decades, starting in elementary school and continuing through our time at James Fenimore Cooper Middle School, where we encountered the characters and experiences that would later appear in our literary works. Castillo displayed his journalistic instincts early on, writing for the *Hawkeye* student newspaper before honing his skills as News Editor for *El Nopal* at Sidney Lanier High School and later as a freelancer for Hearst newspapers.

We reconnected in the mid-1970s during our college years, and then again in graduate school when Castillo was invited to edit a newsletter called *ViAztlan*, which evolved into a full-fledged international journal. His invitation for me to join as co-editor provided me with the opportunity to write stories and articles during a period when magazines and journals flourished alongside the Chicano student movement's opposition to the Vietnam War. Literature was popular. Young people were reading everywhere during this time—every barrio had budding poets or painters, and literary text production became a way to build an intellectual community and express political views.

The Language of Sparrows and Stories marks a significant contribution to American short fiction, offering stories that explore mythology, transformation, auto-memoir, and traditional cuentos. The collection demonstrates considerable literary skill, employing a range of narrative styles, from straightforward realism to works that subtly incorporate irony and satire. Castillo uses the classical ideas of pathos and bathos wisely, employing these emotional tones to enhance rather than manipulate his stories.

The collection's title story, "The Language of Sparrows," showcases Castillo's ambitious scope by weaving Aztec mythology, dream imagery, and reflections on the profound cultural loss experienced by indigenous peoples across the Americas. The story functions as both an artistic achievement and a historical reckoning, confronting the "deadly collision" between indigenous civilizations and European conquistadors. Instead of just documenting loss, Castillo examines how ancient stories and symbols can offer frameworks for understanding modern experiences.

Stories such as "Big Lucas Aka Tonina Jackson," "Short Life," and "House of the Dead" have attracted attention from ethnographers, folklorists, and historians for their accurate portrayal of Tejano experiences during times of cultural homogenization and forced assimilation. These stories reveal the often-hidden ways that culture is coerced, including the use of language as a weapon and the psychological impact of systematic alienation from one's roots. Interestingly, Castillo demonstrates how the very tools of acculturation—literacy, formal education, and fluency in dominant cultural codes—can be harnessed as means of resistance and rebellion. This idea resonates with the life of Malcolm X, who transformed from Malcolm Little through the emancipatory power of literacy and close reading to become a major voice in the liberation movement.

The depiction of barrio life is clear in stories like "The Short Happy Life of Julian Caliente," "A Winter's Tale," "Reader and Advisor," and "Promises to Keep." These stories give readers genuine insights into community dynamics, family ties, and the daily balancing act between tradition and modernity that defines the Mexican American experience. At the same time, there are stories like "Frankie and Carly," "Digital Natives of the City of Light," and "Marfa Lights" that are spun in a light-hearted parody of O. Henry, echoing the tempo of Ernest Hemingway and the pop fantasy of Rod Sterling.

The Language of Sparrows and Stories continues a fictional universe depicting a world that may never exist in the same way again—a world shaped by specific historical events, cultural negotiations, and community dynamics that younger generations might only know through literature or television drama. Rather than merely evoking nostalgia, Castillo's work serves as both preservation and transformation, keeping these experiences vivid and accessible to contemporary readers, demonstrating how traditional storytelling can address universal human concerns. These stories are the lasting marks of history that can never be denied or forgotten. They also affirm that the best regional literature transcends its geographical boundaries to illuminate broader truths about identity, belonging, and the ongoing process of cultural creation.

In a time when assaults on diversity and literary equity in

American literature are increasing and erasing voices, Castillo's work stands as both a historical record and a living testimony that the American short story tradition remains lively when it fully embraces the complexity of the American experience.

Julian S. Garcia is an independent researcher and writer. His articles, fiction, and reviews have appeared in *Regeneración, Puentes, Saguaro Review, Caracol, VíaAztlán, Texas State Historical Association,* and Hearst newspapers.

THE LANGUAGE OF SPARROWS

*H*ernán dreams of flying with sparrows. The dreams are so realistic that he joins them in flight, flapping his wings against the moonlight, watching their dangling stringy legs—the night air breezes against his feathers. The sparrows fly higher, and Hernán flaps harder to join them. Suddenly, a bright light below distracts him. He breaks formation and swooshes toward it at breakneck speed and crashes against a window. He tumbles to the ground, his heart palpitating as a giant hand lifts him.

An ancient and familiar voice whispers words in a language he doesn't understand yet somehow knows: "Nextlaoaloia," it says. "The debt remains unpaid."

Seconds later, his bed trembles, and Hernán opens his eyes.

Touching his chest, he feels a chill, like a shadow passing over him. He traces a finger over the small birthmark on his sternum, a reddish-brown stain shaped vaguely like a bird in flight. It's been there his whole life; this mark his mother had called "la marca del conquistador"—though she would never explain why. The dream seems embarrassingly juvenile, leaving him with an unshakable sense of foreboding.

He gets up and peeks out the window. Sparrows have abandoned the elm trees, and the grass is turning brown. Everything looks grayish and muggy. Cumulus clouds drift northward as hundreds of grackles perch on the powerlines, shrouding the landscape. Another migraine begins to form behind his left eye —the same one that has plagued him on and off since childhood, always accompanied by flashes of visions: stone temples, blood on white stone, screaming birds.

What is the source of his dreams?

He grins when he sees the culprit, a yellow paperback face down on his nightstand. He grabs the novel and shoves it into a drawer. Poor Kafka: everyone's scapegoat. But deep down, he knows it's not Kafka causing these dreams. Something older. Something in his blood, perhaps. Hernán gets dressed and heads to McDonald's for his usual breakfast. His girlfriend Alicia is finishing her night shift at the hospital, and he has texted her. They have been dating steadily for two months, and he's hesitant to share the bird dream with her.

When she arrives, Alicia pecks him on the cheek and sits beside him. They sip coffee and eat sausage biscuits while she chats about the ER. As she reaches for the salt, he notices a thin bracelet of woven red thread around her wrist, decorated with tiny obsidian beads—something he hadn't seen her wear before.

He finally confesses his strange dream, including the voice and odd words. When he mentions "Nextlaoaloia," her eyes widen slightly before her expression stabilizes. She listens carefully to every detail, even the part about the giant hand. She finds it weird but explains.

"Are you afraid of flying? Maybe you're afraid of heights," she asks.

"No, that's not it. I've jumped out of planes before in the military."

"Maybe it's a warning."

She pauses and looks embarrassed, as if she said something

inappropriate. They are both recovering from failed relationships. Hernán sees her pupils dilate, and then she bites her lower lip, as if she's hesitating, afraid to reveal her feelings. She is worried he might think she's weird.

"My grandma always believed in the old ways, saying that when men dreamt of birds, it was because they were being watched." She pauses and wishes she could take back her comment.

"By whom—a jealous girlfriend?"

She blushes. "I don't believe it myself."

There is a long pause, then she throws her head back as if trying to shake off an opposing thought and says unblinkingly that someone has cast a hex on him. The ancient bird woman is coming after him. The words tumble out, and she looks ashamed, staring at her coffee as if she feels she's said too much. Her mind races through ideas, wondering what made her say such things.

"I'm sorry. That's so foolish," she says.

Hernán stares at her wistfully and places his hand over hers comfortingly.

"Don't worry, babe."

They change topics, and he tucks his dream away as just a weird episode. Sometimes, he feels like he's gone through this in another life, a recurring episode of repressed dreams. Later that evening, Hernán raises the subject again and asks her for specificity about what her grandmother believed. She laughs nervously. She feels a connection to his life and shares everything about her background with him. She tells him the bird creature is known as *La Lechuza* (the Screech Owl woman), who hunts stray men. The creature rose after the Conquest of Mexico and the fall of Tenochtitlan when Moctezuma, the mighty Huey tlatoani of the Triple Alliance, was slaughtered by Cortés and his conquistadores. She tells him that Cortés and his bandits garroted the poor emperor. But before dying,

Moctezuma issued a deadly prophecy, cursing Cortés and his future progeny.

"The curse was specific," Alicia says, her voice dropping to almost a whisper. "Moctezuma prophesied that for thirteen generations, the bloodline of Cortés would prosper, gaining wealth and power. But each generation would bear a mark—la marca del conquistador—and be visited by dreams of birds. In the thirteenth generation, a daughter of Texcoco would find the marked one and complete the cycle. The debt would be repaid."

Hernán laughs nervously. "That's quite a story. How do you know all this?"

Alicia's face becomes serious. She recognizes this because she is a direct descendant of the Texcoco and Tlacopan tribes, including the mushroom growers of Culhuacan on the south shore. Her great-grandparents passed down stories and legends of their Aztec ancestors and the wealthy empires they had once ruled. The tales felt more like fairy tales than history to her, but she loved listening to them.

"My grandmother could recite the entire lineage of Cortés," she says. "From Hernán himself to his son Martin, then to his grandson Fernando, and so on. She knew all the names and how they died. Most are asleep, peacefully. But with each generation, the dreams grew stronger."

She remembers reading about Egyptian myths where maidens turn into snakes and birds. She says her mother repeated the fascinating stories of whistling bird women who hovered above treetops, preying on men. Sometimes, she said, they sought comfort with men. Even her grandmother prophesied that she would one day sacrifice her lover, "Leecha, your destiny is near!"

"Leecha, what's that?" Hernán asks. The word strikes terror in his soul because of its familiar sound, as if sparrow friends have told him such tales.

Alicia flushes and tells him that her grandma named her Leecha.

"Oh my. I forgot to tell you, that's my nickname." By strange coincidence, the sound of Alicia's nickname, Leecha, is so close to Lechuza.

A few days go by, and Hernán dreams about sparrows again, but he doesn't tell Alicia. She's out of town, so he decides to visit his friend Gonzalo Sandoval to talk about Alicia and share the story of La Lechuza. After a long talk, Sandoval wants to meet Alicia, whom Hernán has kept hidden from his closest friends since his last breakup with Marina. Sandoval smiles and says, "That friend of yours is projecting."

"What do you mean?"

"It's a Freudian term that means extending one's baser feelings outward."

"Come on, Gonzalo. You don't expect me to believe that nonsense."

"You asked, and I gave my opinion."

Sandoval is an upfront guy with no hidden agenda. He is as close to a brother as possible because both have made great sacrifices for the American Empire. Hernán confides everything in him. They've been friends since Operation Desert Storm, when they joined the Army using the buddy system. Gonzalo graduated from college with a degree in psychology and believes he is providing his friend with a professional assessment.

When Alicia returns from visiting relatives in Mexico, Hernán takes her to Sandoval's house. A woman named Robin is there. She is Sandoval's soulmate; they have been friends with Hernán since high school.

Sandoval is wearing a blue turtleneck and smoking a briar pipe, while Robin sports a tight, red velvet dress with her black hair styled in a pyramid shape. They've been drinking, with Sandoval nursing a Scotch and Robin sipping Dom Perignon.

She hears the doorbell and rushes to answer the front door. Robin looks surprised, her owl eyes widening, dropping her champagne glass.

"Oopsie," Robin utters, embarrassed. "How clumsy of me."

She squats to pick up the broken shards and throws them in a trash can.

"I hope we're not too early?" Hernán says. Then, almost forgetting, he adds, "Oh, Robin. This is Alicia, the girl I told you about." Robin surveys her casually, offering a carefree smile. Alicia, dressed in a gray pullover with a feathered shawl, extends her hand to greet her. But Robin ignores her, turns around, and hugs Hernán. She turns around and shakes Alicia's hand as an afterthought.

They follow Robin into the living room, and Sandoval rises from the sofa, turns off the TV, and asks if they want drinks from the bar. His bar is fully stocked and always open. An awkward silence lingers between Sandoval and Alicia, as if they knew each other from another time. He's seen her somewhere before, but cannot recall where, as if her face is a blurred memory of lost time. During the get-together, Robin and Alicia started on an icy note, as if something had ruffled their feathers, even though the evening was meant to be a formal introduction. "What was your last name again?" Sandoval asks, staring at her face.

"Texcoco," she answers. "Alicia Texcoco."

"Interesting name," Robin interjects. "Spanish?"

"Indigenous," Alicia corrects. "My family has kept our tribal name."

Sandoval appears uneasy. He looks at a framed photo on his bookshelf—Hernán's grandfather standing next to his own, both in military uniforms. The name "Castillo-Cortez" is visible on Hernán's grandfather's uniform.

Sandoval fixes two dry martinis, gives Hernán one, and offers Alicia one.

"No thanks," Alicia says.

"How about tea or a soft drink?"

"A Bloody Mary would be nice," Alicia adds.

Sandoval turns to Robin as if asking to get her a drink. Robin smirks and utters, "No worries, I can make that. Bloody things are my specialty."

That evening, alcohol gets the better of them. Robin conducts a hawkish inquiry, asking about Alicia's ancestry, while Sandoval hints that she is hiding something about her past. She senses that Alicia's lineage is linked to a tragic ending that may conflict with Hernán, but she cannot be certain. After a while, the visiting couple excuses themselves and leaves. Hernán is deeply embarrassed by the whole episode. On the way home, Alicia keeps silent until she asks, "Well, did I pass their test?"

"Don't mind them. Sandoval is just overprotective. I saved his life in Iraq."

"And Robin."

"She's like a big sister to me."

"She's attracted to you."

"Don't be ridiculous," Hernán says, dodging her question.

They stop talking, and he turns on the radio. Peggy Lee is singing "Is That All There Is," and he says, "Ain't that the truth!" They turn to each other and laugh. The evening is forgotten as a muddled, nightmare-like experience.

When they get home, Alicia leaves the passenger side of the car with the house keys, ready to open the front door, while he drives the car into the garage. When he turns off the ignition and gets out, she comes to the driver's side with a concerned look and says, "This is not good."

"What's wrong?"

She asks him to follow her to the entrance, then points to a dead bird lying near the hedges.

"This is a bad omen. It's a red crowned sparrow."

"Let me go in and get a Zip-Lock," Hernán says.

He unlocks the front door and goes inside. She waits outside, protecting the dead bird from their neighbor's cat. The wind picks up, and the trees rustle with chirping birds alarmed at the scene. With the inside of the bag, he picks up the lifeless thing with the tips of his fingers and reverses the plastic bag.

Hernán tells her sparrows sometimes lose their bearings and crash into windows. Seeing a dead bird near the entryway is nothing ominous. And here, almost like a trance, Alicia reveals another part of her past. She tells him she can read the entrails of birds to decipher their meanings. They look at each other incredulously. Alicia shakes her head, wondering why she even said that. She is openly candid about everything.

"You're joking," he says.

She is serious. As a child, Alicia was fascinated by how toys worked, often dismantling them and dissecting frogs and birds. She explains that the red-crowned sparrow holds special significance in Aztec mythology because, when the ancient tribes of Mesoamerica fell, hundreds of dead red-crowned sparrows rained from the sky. The priests of Texcoco recognized it as a bad omen and a sign that their empire was collapsing. Her grandmother taught her the art of prophecy by reading a bird's entrails. He is beginning to enjoy the intrigue.

"Let's do it," Hernán says.

Alicia darts into the bathroom to grab gloves from the bottom of the medicine cabinet and opens the garage door. She carries the bag to a workbench that runs along the wall. Wearing her gloves, she removes the bird from the Ziplock bag and places it flat on a worktable. She adjusts a gooseneck light on the workbench and switches it on. The bright light floods the dead sparrow, revealing its puffed breast. She takes a sharp-pointed bone knife and slices open the chest. To their surprise, the tiny heart is still beating. Hernán is stunned and amazed.

As a nurse, Alicia is familiar with surgical tools and assisting

ER doctors, observing how carefully they open a cavity. He sees her dissecting the breast, whispering to it, pulling out stringy parts, and tossing them into the air. She lifts the tiny heart in her hand. When the viscera fall to the floor, they look like an assortment of hieroglyphs only she can decipher.

"What are you whispering?"

She says softly, "It's the language of sparrows."

This is madness, he thinks, as he uncovers a stranger side of her. Something is disgusting about the whole situation, and Hernán feels bile rising from his stomach.

"What's your full name, Hernán?" she asks suddenly, eyes still fixed on the bird's entrails.

"You know my name," he says, confused.

"Your complete name. Your family name."

He hesitates. "Hernán Gabriel Castillo. Why?"

"No other names? Nothing your family dropped over the years?"

The question strikes him as strange. There was something — a hyphenated Spanish name his father had mentioned once. Something old-fashioned. But they removed it when they came to America. But how could she know that?

"Castillo is fine," he says firmly.

Alicia intently studies the sparrow's viscera, then utters, "Robin is involved with a coven of Lechuzas. She's not who she claims to be. She knows what you are. They're trying to protect you."

He is speechless. This was way out of line.

"Now, wait a doggone minute."

Hernán firmly states this is nonsense. Alicia remains resolute. She shakes her head and says men do not understand the forces of nature that have governed them for thousands of years. He stays silent and leaves the room, while Alicia stays behind to clean up the mess. They change clothes and go to bed. She becomes playful and wants to apologize.

That night, they have the best sex in months. She is utterly nurturing. Hernán feels like crawling into her uterus and nestling into her womb. As they lie entangled, she traces her fingers over the birthmark on his chest—the mark he'd rarely shown anyone.

"La marca del conquistador," she whispers, almost to herself.

"What did you say?" he asks drowsily.

"Nothing, my love. Just admiring you."

He notices the red thread bracelet is gone from her wrist. Instead, a thin strand is wound around her finger, as if being measured. He is tired and wants to sleep. As he drifts off, his phone buzzes. A text from Sandoval says, "Call me tomorrow. I found something about your family you should know."

He doesn't respond, already half-asleep. He gets text messages and attachments from Sandoval and discovers a cache of immigration documents.

After that night, the dreams of sparrows grow more vivid. Hernán sees more dead birds in the following months. He studies the old family photos and documents—his father's birth certificate showing the hyphenated "Castillo-Cortez," genealogy papers his grandmother kept, and a family tree tracing back to Spain and Mexico. The "s" in Cortés mysteriously changed to "z." Then, one night, after a fulfilling, tiring day, Hernán falls into REM sleep. It's marvelous. He sleeps in the fetal position. In his dream, Leecha overpowers him with enormous, feathered wings. She has glowing green eyes and feeds him with her red beak. A spaghetti-like worm dangled before him. He opens his mouth and sticks out his small tongue.

That morning, he tells her about the recurring dream of sparrows. Alicia smiles and tells him she loves him and will never fly away. He pauses, smiles, and repeats the exciting line, "Never fly away, heh." She laughs, denying having said such a thing. Alicia says she did not say those words, but he insists she did. He sighs, shrugging it off, and goes about his business.

That evening, she texts him, saying she is running late and trying to clock out before the night crew arrives. The heavy influx of ER patients has subsided. They are supposed to go to a nice restaurant. He gets dressed when he hears a loud thud; something hits the bay window. He draws open the curtains and sees a smudge on the windowpane. Not another sparrow. He rushes downstairs, opens the front door, and looks around the hedges. He finds another dead bird. He picks it up and sees its limp neck. Dark, lifeless eyes peer at him, and he feels a strange kinship with the poor animal. He places the dead bird in a plastic bag and shoves it into the trash can. He doesn't tell Alicia about the dead sparrow, fearing she might want to do surgery.

That night, they go to the Riverwalk and have a spaghetti meal with red wine at Luigi's. When they get home, they rip off their clothes and make greedy love. Afterward, Hernán sleeps like a baby, dreaming again of being a bird. He glides the jet stream, soaring capably above treetops. Suddenly, he sees a glowing light beckoning him. He flies straight to it, slams against a windowpane, and falls. A giant hand is lifting him. Enormous pain radiates from his chest. He opens his eyes and sees Leecha caressing him. Her hand clutches an obsidian blade so close to him that all fears disappear. Do not be alarmed, she whispers, for sparrows are responsible for carrying souls into the other world.

In his dream, Hernán lay on a granite slab the size of a surgical table atop the Templo Mayor, his chest open, his trembling heart ready to feel the full impact of the Quinto Sol. Leecha wears a plumed green headdress, holding a sacrificial knife, standing atop the pyramid. Around them, thirteen sparrows sit in a perfect circle, observing. She raises the obsidian blade high.

"The thirteenth generation," she chants. "The debt must be repaid."

He notices a red thread wrapped around his heart,

measuring it carefully. The birthmark on his chest—la marca del conquistador—shines with an otherworldly glow. In a moment of perfect clarity, he remembers everything: the family stories his grandmother whispered, the documents hidden in his father's safe, the lineage traced through centuries. Now he understands why his family changed their name from Castillo-Cortez to Castillo, why they moved so often, and why his father warned him to stay away from women with "old world eyes."

"Nextlaoaloia," Leecha says. "The seeker has found what he seeks."

She is about to fulfill the prophecy of the Huey Tlatoani. Alicia mumbles the language of sparrows and cuts out his heart. He never wakes up from his sparrow dream, even as Alicia tries desperately to resuscitate him. On the nightstand, the family tree he found earlier that day lies open, tracing his lineage to Hernán Cortés. Hernán is the thirteenth generation in the Hernán Cortés lineage. He is the great-great-great-grandson, ten times removed from Martin Cortés, son of Hernán Cortés, who died in his sleep.

In the morning light, a red-crowned sparrow perches on the windowsill, watching. The debt has been repaid, and the prophecy has been fulfilled.

THE LAST TIME

$\mathcal{T}$he last time I saw my father was in downtown San Antonio, by the Riverwalk, on the corner of E. Commerce and Navarro St. I was coming from New York City, where I had a one-bedroom apartment on Amsterdam Ave, within walking distance of the university where I was a sophomore.

I called his office and arranged to meet him. I hadn't been home in quite a while. My father was a stranger to me. My mother had separated from him decades ago, and I hadn't seen him since then, but as soon as I saw him sitting on a bench, I knew he was my father, my kin, my flesh and blood, my inexorable destiny. I knew that when I grew up, I would be somewhat like him, and I would need to plan my outings with fewer aggressive restrictions.

He was a bondsman with Donovan & Donovan, a small three-person firm that served low-income, struggling offenders who needed bail bonds and notary signatures. He was a sharp-dressed man, often wearing white shirts with dark ties and suits by Hart Schaffner Marx.

I was glad to see him again. He tapped me on the back and shook my hand.

"Hi, Joey," he said. "I'd take you to my favorite restaurant, but it's far away. I know you don't like to wait, and I have an appointment in Austin later today. Very busy, you know." He was so close to me that I could smell enough whisky on his breath to make a small boy dizzy. It was a mishmash of unfiltered cigarettes, Old Spice, and the scent of shoe polish that conspired on a male inching closer to middle age.

We visited an old, established restaurant on the Riverwalk, which is typically crowded with tourists. He signaled to a waiter and skipped the hostess who was about to take our names. It was still too early for tourists and late enough for the regular crowd.

"If you want something badly, don't wait," he muttered.

We took a booth. We saw a chubby waiter arguing with a busser, and then my father hailed the waiter loudly. "Pancho!" he shouted. "*Hombre, Camarada!* You!" His boisterousness was turning heads and seemed out of place. "Hello, could we have some service here!" he shouted. "Pronto!" Then he snapped his fingers. This caught the chubby waiter's attention, and he shuffled over to our booth.

"Were you snapping your fingers at me?" he asked.

"Calm down, calm down, beef-master," my father said. "If you can muster the strength—and if it wouldn't be too much above your service duty, we would like a couple of dry martinis —shaken, not stirred."

"I don't appreciate you snapping your fingers, sir".

"Okay, I should have brought my foghorn," my father said. "You know I have a foghorn just for thick, foggy places like this for old tugboat waiters who can barely see the shoreline. Now, take your little pad and pencil and see if you can get this straight: two very dry martinis shaken, not stirred. Repeat after me: two dry martinis shaken, not stirred."

"I think it's best you go somewhere else," the waiter said quietly.

"That lard master," my father uttered, "is the most brilliant suggestion I have ever heard. Come, Joey, we'll get out of this two-bit hellhole."

I followed my father out to another restaurant. He was not so boisterous this time. He ordered our dry martinis. Our drinks came, and then he cross-examined me about the football season and whether Joe Namath was a better quarterback than Johnny Unitas. I had no idea who these players were, and I could tell he needed another drink, so he stuck the edge of the table with his Martini glass, making a ping-ping sound, and began shouting again, "*Hombre! Pancho! Camarada!* You!"

"Could we trouble you to bring us two of the same when you have the time?"

"How old is the boy?" the waiter asked.

"That my little lackey is none of your goddam business."

"I'm sorry, sir," the waiter said. "I cannot serve the boy another drink."

"Well, it's Howdy Doody time! I wouldn't take another lousy drink from this place if it were free. Come, Joey, there are better restaurants than this sewer-swill of a place."

He tossed a twenty, and we left. I followed him out of the restaurant into another one. Here, the servers wore red jackets with initials. It looked rather expensive, featuring pictures of bullfighters, bull heads, and lavish portraits of local celebrities. We sat down, and my father began to shout again.

"Hello, *hombre. Toro! Toro! Servicio, por favor.* Can we get something here instead of all this bull crap staring at us from these walls? Hello, *señor! El Toro señor!* Can we trouble you to bring us two very dry Martinis, shaken, not stirred? Pronto! Not mañana!"

"*Si, si, si.* Two dry Martinezes," the waiter snickered.

"You know damn well what I want," my father growled. "I

want two dry Martinis and make it snappy. Things have changed in the land of bulls and frozen margaritas. So, my friend El Presidente tells me. Let's see what Mexico can produce in the way of a civilized cocktail."

"This isn't Mexico," the waiter said.

"Don't argue with me," my father said. "Just do as you're told."

"I just thought you might know this isn't Mexico, and I'm not a matador," the waiter said.

"There's one thing I can't tolerate," my father said. "It's an impudent waiter. Come on, Joey."

The fourth place we went was an Italian restaurant on the River Walk.

"*Buon giorno*," my father said. "*For favore, possiamo avere due* Martini cocktails, *forti, forti. Molto gin, poco vermut.*"

"I don't speak Italian," the waiter said.

"For crying out loud," my father said. "What type of joint is this? You understand Italian, and you know God-damn well you do. *Vogliamo due Martini cocktails Subito!*" The waiter left us and spoke with the head maitre'd, who came over to our table and said, "I'm sorry, sir. But this table is reserved."

"All right," my father said. "Get us another table."

"All tables are reserved," the head maitre'd said.

"I get it," my father said. "You don't desire our patronage. My lira isn't good enough for this stinking two-bit imitation of a restaurant. The hell with you all. Vada al inferno. Let's go, Joey."

"I have to get my plane," I said.

"I'm sorry, sonny," my father said. "I'm sorry." He put his arms around me and pressed me against him. "I'll get a taxi for you. If there had only been time to go to my favorite restaurant, the Mexican Manhattan."

"That's all right, pop," I said.

"I'll get you a newspaper," he said. "That's it. I'll get you something to read on the plane."

Then he went to a corner newsstand and said, "Excuse me, kind sir, will you be good enough to favor me with one of your god-damned, no-good, two-bit afternoon papers?" The clerk ignored him and stared at a magazine cover. "Is it asking too much, kind sir?" my father said, "Is it asking too much for you to sell me one of your disgusting rags of yellow journalism?"

"I have to go, Dad," I said. "It's late."

"Now, just wait a second, Joey," he said. "Just wait a second. I want to get a rise from this fellow."

"Goodbye, Dad," I said. I went up the stairs from the River-walk, hailed a yellow cab, and left for New York. I saw my father sitting at an outdoor bar, drinking another Martini.

That was the last time I saw my father.

A WINTER'S TALE

*I*t had been decades since I saw him, my father. The last time was when I traveled to San Antonio and met him at the Riverwalk. He had gotten plastered on Martinis, and his behavior left a sour taste in my mouth. Stranger things have happened in my life.

That winter was the darkest period of my life. Belinda, my partner, was in the living room while I was in the study, listening to Beethoven's "Pastoral" and re-reading Fyodor Dostoevsky's *The Brothers Karamazov* because I intended to teach the novel at the start of the new semester. The music gave me a false sense of security.

I found it challenging to reread a work of great sentimentality because Old Man Karamazov reminded me so much of my father that I was not particularly fond of the first chapter when I read it in high school. Twenty years had passed since I last saw him shouting at servers in restaurants on the Riverwalk and making a fool of himself; I had repressed many of our arguments because they gave me ambivalent feelings about myself. Every time I read a passage in which Old Man Karamazov makes a fool of himself in front of Father Zossima, I see my father in the background, wobbling drunk, shouting at the top of his lungs that life had cheated him, and that the world was unfair. Had Father Zossima existed, he would have been appalled by my father's antics.

Belinda interrupted me as I sat reading, allowing my mind to drift aimlessly to the cold, barren landscape of Czarist Russia. She brought me some freshly brewed coffee and cinnamon cake.

"Having fun, dear?" she asked.

The twinkle in her eyes made me relax, as she always had a cheerful disposition. And she always put me in a festive mood, even when my spirits were down. All morning, I had this strange feeling within, almost oppressing my better self. I felt like an expectant father waiting for the moment when the truth came bursting forth, staring me in the face. I placed the book down and reached for a slice of cake, allowing me to delay my obligatory assignment. Besides, it was a welcome respite.

The afternoon gave way to twilight. Belinda was about to sit in her favorite lounge chair to read the Sunday Times, a weekly ritual she did exquisitely by rote. Since grad school, she had become an avid reader of the arts section, followed by the magazine, and the Book Review.

I picked up the Opinion section and browsed indiscriminately through it. Then, I glanced at the letters to the editor section, looking for editorial banter sent by pedantic readers who flaunted their erudition. Unfortunately, there was no such stuff today.

At that instance, we heard the melodic chime of the doorbell. We looked at one another. Belinda grabbed her purse, flipped out her appointment book, and glanced at the calendar; she hadn't penciled in anybody for the day.

"Who could that be?" I uttered.

I wouldn't say I liked any company on Sundays, particularly those who dropped by without calling or checking to see if we were busy with other things.

She smiled and said, "I'll get it, dear. Get back to Siberia."

I returned to my reading, still feeling a bit uneasy about the evening and wondering if I should exercise or go out back to chop some wood—anything to escape Old Man Karamazov.

A few minutes later, Belinda returned with a pale expression, her eyes a bit watery, her beautiful porcelain face etched with dread and anxiety. She bit her lower lip and gave me a strange, faraway look. The last time she looked at me like that was when she smashed the car bumper.

"Well," I asked.

She forced a slight smile as though repressing something, but I could see pain in her bright eyes.

Startled, I set the novel aside and hugged her, "What's wrong, sweetheart? You look like you've just seen a ghost."

"I have."

She was initially hesitant to share this with me. Her tone conveyed caution, and her voice was carefully controlled with pauses and momentary lapses. She gazed at me for a long time and sighed as if she were looking at a wounded sparrow. She hugged me tightly, and I could feel a slight tremor, a sense of nervousness.

Belinda did not know how I would react to the news because, after seeing photos of him and hearing so much about him, she had instantly recognized my father. The look in her eyes betrayed agony and desperation. I had long ago told her that my father left for Mexico, abandoning my mother and seven children to the mercy of AFDC. The acronym stood for Aid for Families with Dependent Children. The dreaded "W" word. We were welfare kids, and the term then carried a degree of shame, a stamp of defeat on our foreheads. I was spared the humiliation and trauma when my grandparents assumed guardianship because I was under ten.

My brothers and sisters weren't so fortunate. When my mother passed away from a brain aneurysm the following year, they were left, like wild cubs, to fend for themselves. My older brother joined the Army and harbored a deep resentment toward both our parents, while the next oldest, a successful entrepreneur, became indifferent and assumed another identity. My sisters weren't so fortunate. Like butterflies, they flew their separate ways.

"Honey," she paused. "I think it's your father."

The word "father" came hurling toward me like a brick against a windowpane. Maybe I had misunderstood her, and she meant father, as in priest.

"It's your father," she repeated.

The word was unmistakably clear. She repeated it, and there was no doubt: history was confronting me. My father had returned in a Winnebago, no less—my long-lost dad, a man exiled from memory.

The image of him, blurry like a sepia photograph, peering down at me with bloodshot eyes, a sardonic grin, and a Martini in one hand, reopened old wounds. I was suspended in time, and a flashback of adolescence reared its ugly head. After looking me up in the phone directory, my old man jotted down my address and came knocking at my door. It's all calculatingly simple.

"What shall I tell him?" she asked.

I nodded and said point-blank: "I don't want to see him. Tell him anything. For Pete's sake, tell him I'm not home."

Belinda crossed her arms, arched an eyebrow, and protested. "Joey, I'm ashamed of you. What kind of man did I marry? Go to him. He's your father."

Even upset, Belinda looked stunningly beautiful. Her Dutch

boy haircut, complemented by thick, dark eyebrows and razor-sharp Smith College wit, made her highly perceptive. She wasn't going to budge. We exchanged glances and said nothing until I reconsidered my stance and acquiesced. She was right. What kind of man would I be to turn him away—no better than him, I guess.

"Tell him I'll be right out."

She hugged me and kissed my cheek. "I knew you'd come to your senses, darling. That's why I married you."

I wanted him to wait, just as I had waited. I swallowed the last ounce of coffee; it had a bitter, almost salty taste. Despite the wintry evening, I was sweating. She led him into the living room while I waited in the study, contemplating what to tell him and wondering what he might say to me. I reflected on my mother and how long she had suffered, and then I thought about my brothers and what a raw deal they had gotten in life.

Opening the door just a crack, I peeked at the stranger—my father—sitting on the sofa. He appeared incredibly frail, with a thin, haggard face framed by steel-rimmed spectacles. Reading the local paper and dressed in dark wine corduroys, a black turtleneck, and a tweed jacket, my father was likely pondering what he would tell me. His jet-black hair had turned gray.

He rose from the sofa when I walked into the living room. Our eyes locked, and we stood frozen momentarily like two enemy soldiers in a barren landscape, each waiting for some sign of resignation. Who would blink first? Up close, he appeared pale, almost ill.

I blinked. "Hello," I said.

"*Mijo,*" he uttered in Spanish, the syllables faintly audible, as if unsure of their meaning, straining to release the foreign word that meant "son" from the solitude of memory. Even the language felt distant because I had long forsaken the mother tongue of my ancestors. It was like a perfect stranger approaching and uttering a filial expression. We shook hands firmly. His dark eyes became dewy and moist, and then he surprised me with an abrazo, a strong hug. I felt the mist of his whisky breath. Why had he suddenly remembered he had a son? My wife stood there quietly.

"Ahh... this is Belinda," I said.

"Yes, honey. We've met. Listen, I'll let you two get re-acquainted. I'm sure you and your father have much to discuss," she said.

"Long time," I stammered. "So, what brings you to New York?" That was stupid. The words came out without even thinking. I wanted to hurt him for all the miserable years of suffering. Wrinkles furrowed deeply into his face, and the scent of musk and cigarette smoke clung about his coat. He looked emaciated. Perhaps all the heavy smoking finally caught up with him.

Feeling my passive aggressiveness, he smiled and said apologetically, "Yes. Quite a long time." His eyes were downcast. He understood my icy reception as the penalty for his long-term absence. What did he expect—a ticker-tape parade? I wanted him to feel shame. I knew he had returned to the mother country. The gulf of silence between us grew larger, and then I asked, not knowing what to say, "How are things in Mexico?" It was a foolish question. I wasn't sure what I meant by it or why I had even asked it. I only knew that when things got bad in the United States, it had a trickle-down effect, making things worse in Mexico.

"Nothing much. People are poorer than before. The ranch grandfather left is nothing more than a ten-acre patch with squatters now. There is nothing. The land is sterile..." He paused in mid-sentence. He looked blankly at me as if he had forgotten some part of himself, his wallet, maybe. The look reminded me of the time Belinda and I traveled halfway to Canada, only to remember she had left the back porch door unlocked. It was something like that.

"Anna! My Anna is outside!" he blurted.

"Who?"

He looked embarrassed and said, "I have someone with me."

"May I?" he inquired.

"Of course. By all means."

He excused himself and bolted out the door. Belinda poked her head out from the kitchen and asked if everything was fine.

"Making progress, honey?"

"He forgot to bring in his girlfriend," I said.

"Oh my."

I looked at her, shrugged my shoulders, and suppressed my anger; he had a woman with him. Such a brazen act was all too typical of him. He was always one to do as he pleased.

"What should I do?" I asked,

"Invite her in, silly," she said.

The other woman waited, braving the cold, inside a Winnebago. Minutes later, they entered the house and settled comfortably by the fireplace.

"So, you're Joey. How nice to meet ya."

Her name was Anna Tobermann. She was a tall brunette in her fifties, with a slight foreign accent. They had met while traveling; she was a retired accountant who had gone to Mexico for excitement and relaxation, only to meet the playboy of the Western world. They had fallen in love. He appeared more animated now that she stood beside him, and she resembled a starry-eyed schoolgirl. It was unbearable to watch them. He fished in his coat pocket and pulled out a pack of Luckies, tapped them on his palm, retrieved a cigarette, and lit it. Then he remembered he was a guest somewhere, not some landed gentry in his hacienda.

"Oh, how careless of me. Do you mind?"

"It's all right," I said. After his first puff, he began coughing irritably like those phlegm-throated winos.

"Damned things will be the death of me," he said, coughing.

"We have to learn to make sacrifices, don't we?" I replied. At this point, Belinda entered the room, and I introduced her to Anna, his girlfriend, who became lively and friendly.

"I've told Joe so many times it's going to be the death of him. But he won't listen to me. Perhaps you can get some sense into him."

"Me? Why should he listen to me?" I asked.

"Why should he listen to you? You know, you're his favorite son," she said, flashing her teeth. The phrase "favorite son" struck me as awkwardly offensive, as though she were mocking me. But clearly, the poor woman didn't know diddley about my life, nor was she privy to all the headaches our broken family had suffered through the years. My father looked at Anna with outrage, as if she had let out the family secrets. I never imagined myself as his favorite anything.

"Is that so?" I asked.

My wife sensed the rising drama and interrupted, "Perhaps a piece of coffee cake and coffee. I've just brewed it."

Anna smiled and offered to help, and they both disappeared into the kitchen.

I stared at him and asked, "So, tell me, to what do I owe this honor?"

He frowned.

"Now, don't get so self-righteous. I've been in Mexico; you should be aware of that. Mexico City, to be exact. I've visited the tombs of our most joyous ancestors. You know we are descendants of the Conquistadors," he said triumphantly. The tone of his voice for a moment reminded me of Lee J. Cobb, the big-boned, burly actor who played Fyodor Karamazov in the film version of the novel, playing the buffoon and feigning pity in front of Father Zossima. It was all revolting. I wanted none of his fantasies, as this was no time for false pride.

"Knock off the bullshit. Just tell me why you've come back? Why me? Just a simple answer. Or shall I ask you both to leave?"

He stared at me, somewhat surprised, as though wondering why he had even bothered to find our house, let alone visit me.

He stared morosely into my eyes while fidgeting with his keys, scratched his head, and said, "Frankly, I don't know. I've wasted my whole life in cantinas searching for answers. I've lost a family, my fortune, and in some way, I've lost the most important thing in my life—my self-respect." He looked defeated, and his words sounded scripted, almost as if he had memorized his lines, prepared to say anything to gain entrance into my life. And that was not going to happen. As he muttered, it became clear that my father was no longer that menacing giant. Frail to the point of weakness, his towering features, once the epitome of stone-faced patriarchal power, had chipped away to a crumbling façade. He was probably dying, and too proud to admit it.

"What about Anna? How does she fit into all this?"

"That's not your concern," he uttered flatly.

He was right. I didn't care about the woman, but I had a right to ask.

Just then, Belinda and Anna returned with a carafe of coffee, plates, and cups, and Anna poured him a cup. "It's hot, honey," she added with caution.

Some oil reproductions in the dining room caught their attention. She got up from the sofa to get a closer look. And then, she turned to me and stared at me momentarily, as though studying me, perhaps, comparing me to my father.

"I understand you went to college here," Anna said.

"Yes, ah, and?"

"The Big Apple," my father interrupted. "He could have gone to Harvard, but he wanted New York." He had kept track of me all those years, tracking my moves like a tagged animal left out in the wild. Noticing that I had not returned her chit-chat, Anna moved, looking at a reproduction hanging in the living room.

"That's a Caravaggio," Belinda said. Anna slipped on her spectacles, which were dangling from her bosom, and said,

"Why, yes. Of course, it is." Father joined her and stared at the baroque painting of David with Goliath's head. He became nervous, his body reflecting impatience. Perhaps he imagined that my next move was to expose the past and the miserable life he had created for his sons and daughters.

He looked at me for a few seconds, moistening his lip, and then uttered, "Son, I'll get right to the point." He wanted to sound forceful, almost businesslike. But some element was missing. He didn't look menacing anymore.

"I'd prefer it."

"I need a thousand dollars," he said, almost like a whisper. Pity and embarrassment shrouded his face. His voice reduced to a whimper. So that was it? The money. He had come this far for the money. I should have known. There he was—a man who said he'd never leave, who mailed us 25 dollars apiece on our birthdays from faraway places and was now asking for it all back with interest.

"What about the others? Have you asked them?"

"They're all closed their doors. You're the last one."

"I see."

He had traveled long distances from Mexico City to San Antonio to New York to borrow money and maybe get one last glimpse of his connection to an abandoned past.

"Are you in some kind of trouble?" I had to ask.

"No," he shook his head, "It's a personal matter."

I thought about my brothers and sisters and then my mother. My anger was mounting. I felt a profound urge to slap him in the face, but from a distance, Belinda looked at me with her doe-like eyes and the do-the-right-thing stare—a long gap of silence. My father was waiting for my answer. The grandfather clock in the hallway ticked away the seconds, transforming them into a past that would soon become a memory. Time was the arbitrator, and I had two choices: one, refuse him the money and tell him exactly how I felt, or two, give him the money and forgive the past. I snapped back from my lapse into the current, looking absent-mindedly into his ebony eyes, and said yes. He wrung his hands and broke down: "Don't worry. I'll pay it all back. I promise."

"Don't worry," I said, without thinking. He probably knew his empty promises meant nothing to me. For a second, I thought about Smerdyakov, the bastard Karamazov son, and how he had faked his seizure after killing his father. It didn't turn out like that.

Belinda turned to me, and I could see in her expression that she wanted me to give him the money. So, I got up from the sofa, left the room, and returned with a King James Bible.

He looked at me with disbelief, knowing that he was irreligious, and said, "Oh, please. Not that, I know what you're thinking."

"No, you don't."

I sat down with the heavy volume and opened it wide. Inside, I withdrew ten crisp hundred-dollar bills from a hidden compartment and placed them in his hands. I wanted to wash my hands and forget the whole ordeal. Paying him would be cathartic, thus severing my obligations to him. I knew he would never repay me.

"You don't know how grateful I am for this."

He stood up and hugged and whispered, "I'm truly sorry, son. For everything. Please forgive me."

I remained silent. Then I uttered, "It is what it is."

He hugged Belinda, and I hugged Anna.

"You're such a charming couple," Anna said. "God bless both of you."

I later learned from Belinda, who had gotten it from Anna, that my father was dying of cancer. My chance to finally right a wrong melted away like snowflakes touching the ground. All those years of pent-up frustration reached an unsatisfactory conclusion, and the final chapter of his life felt particularly poignant, given that I was his favorite son.

There was no hurt, not even betrayal—only an ambivalent sense of closure, you might say. They departed in their bulky Winnebago, lurching down a wooded path until we could no longer see them. That night, snow buried our house—cold, cold snow.

THE SHORT HAPPY LIFE OF
JULIÁN CALIENTE

*W*hen Julián Caliente ended his midnight shift at the local fast-food restaurant, a hot breakfast awaited him at home. He tossed his cap and the dirty work apron into the hamper and clocked out. The manager offered him a customary Snappy Meal, but he declined. He didn't want A Snappy Meal because he'd seen the rat droppings, cockroach feelers, and squashed spiders caught in mixers and in between cooking utensils.

When Teresa heard his car in the driveway, she rushed to open the door.

"Did you eat your free breakfast?"

"I'm tired of eating that crap!" Julián told her.

"You don't have to work there, you know. You can go back to substitute teaching."

"Nah. Not that white-picket-fence bullshit!"

After thirty years of teaching third graders, Julián didn't want anything associated with kids. He was finished with that life. Instead, he chose to clean toilets, take trash to outside bins, and mop floors. It was easy. Working at the fast-food place involved no thinking, just plain manual labor.

"Then stop nagging, for God's sake. No one's making you work," Teresa rebuffed him.

She'd made him buttered toast and sunny-side eggs and opened a Dr. Pepper. After breakfast, he took a dump and showered.

Minutes later, Julián entered the guest bedroom, locked the door, sat at the computer, and logged onto his secret Cloud account. Chapter headings flashed on the screen, and he picked up where he had left off. Julián spent the following hours at the keyboard typing the latest chapter of his cuentos, *Princess Morning Sun*, which tells the story of Native Americans during Spanish colonial rule. He was writing about Fray Don Jose, a Franciscan monk who worked in the missions during the early history of New Spain, before the arrival of European settlers in the New World.

Fray Don Jose was a former priest seeking redemption because he harbored impure thoughts. To exorcise his demons, he flogged himself to chase away those harping demons, which made him seek out young virgins. Here in New Spain, native women were bountiful. To him, they had yet to be baptized and were free to be blessed (a euphemism for the sexual act).

Julián began typing:

FRAY DON JOSE hired a young Indian girl to empty pisspots every morning, clean his room, and prepare the chapel for service. When the soldiers spotted her, they opened the mission doors because the girl, barely thirteen, posed no threat. And Fray Don Jose signaled his approval to the soldiers.

Just the day before, Fray Don Jose had documented two Apache attacks against the Mission because soldiers had raped a tribal daughter. The soldiers reported that the girl had taunted them and was responsible for their actions.

"They're savages. Look at them. No sense of decency, no

moral restraint," Corporal Cruz said. He confessed to Fray Don Jose that he saw her nude demeanor as reprehensible, walking about with exposed breasts. The temptation was too much as the soldiers reported the lovely girl bathing near a creek in full view. She removed her leather tunic, unbraided her hair, stepped into the water, and lathered herself with a foamy cloth. Even Private Aleman, the assistant to Corporal Cruz, reported she was beckoning them by lathering her lovely breasts and bending over, showing them her fleshy bottom. When Cruz and Aleman got closer to her for full inspection, she smiled and stood up, showing her glistening, wet body. Then she lifted her leg near the bank. The girl was taunting them, they argued. And so, they removed their clothes and entered the stream. She was curious about their white bodies. But panicked when Cruz grabbed her breasts and bent her over while Aleman maneuvered himself and splayed her legs. She did not scream but fully participated.

It was consensual, they said.

But that was not precisely what Princess Morning Sun told Chief Soaring Eagle. She claimed the soldiers invited her to a secluded stream and offered her golden beads, pearls, and blankets. When she got closer, the heavy-set soldier, Corporal Cruz, grabbed her hair, twisted it around her neck, and groped her breasts while the other pulled down her leather tunic. She tried to scream, but the fat one covered her mouth. A few minutes later, they relieved themselves until satisfied and left laughing, telling her to return for more.

Ashamed and disgusted, she ran to tell her father. The soldiers had no idea that Morning Sun was the daughter of a chieftain.

"Father, the soldiers dishonored me," she told Chief Soaring Eagle. She wept, telling him the shameful actions of the Spanish soldiers. The Braves heard about the assault and wanted to take immediate action.

"This will not stand," Chief Soaring Eagle said.

She looked at her father and said, "Leave it to me. I will regain my honor!"

A LOUD KNOCK at the door interrupted Julián's narrative. He hated interruptions because they intruded on his writing.

"Whattt!" Julián yelled.

"It's your editor friend. He's outside. Do you want me to tell him you're busy? Or come back another day?" Teresa hollered at the door.

Julián opened the door ajar and said, "No, Teresa. I'll get it." He clicked the computer mouse and saved his file.

His friend Max visited him weekly to discuss his writing progress. A writing teacher at a local college, Max had been his friend since the early days at Our Lady of Guadalupe elementary school, where they were under the tutelage of the savage Brother Hector and the stern hand of Father Parks.

"What's going on? Any new stuff to show me?" Max asked.

"Nothing yet. You interrupted me. I was writing about this horny friar inseminating all the Indian women near the missions."

"That's disgusting. No one will publish it."

"I need money. It's just a draft. I have lots of bills to pay. Besides, I'm using a pen name."

Max shook his head and said, "You must write about lofty things. These stories serve no purpose other than to rile our bodies and shame our souls."

"Oh my God, Max. Do you know who you sound like?"

"Who?"

"Brother Hector. That smart-ass, self-righteous son-of-a-bitch who was quick to judge and slow to forgive. He never forgave us for laughing at that prostitute on Guadalupe Street.

She fell near the crosswalk, and you spotted her red panties, remember?"

Max smirked, saying: "Jesus! You still remember that incident?"

"Yeah. All the kids walking in a single file laughed. Brother Hector gave us a scowl like the wrath of God was coming down on us. We sang Las Mañanitas to a house next to the El Progresso store. Remember, we sang morning songs to the sick people?"

Julián remembered Father Parks asking Brother Hector about Old Lady Puente when they returned to the classroom. She was not good, Brother Hector said, but there were more pressing problems that needed to be rectified. Brother Hector told the priest about the crosswalk incident, the sexual nature of Julián's crime, and how Max had aided in the grievous sin.

Father Parks turned crimson and pointed to the rectory. They marched to the office with Brother Hector behind them, and Sister Philomena took over the classroom.

"Only the wrath of God can cleanse your sins."

"What sins?" Max asked.

"Silence! You little wretch!"

"*Cayate lo hocico!*" Julián quipped.

Brother Hector slapped Julian across the face, shouting, "How dare you speak like that to me!" Julián sneered, "I wasn't talking to you!" Of course, Max knew Julián was lying. It was intended for Brother Hector, the Jesuit wannabe, who believed that suffering and punishment were the keys to salvation.

But Max recalled the incident differently from Julián. It was Julián who whistled at the prostitute, causing the startled woman to lose her footing while crossing the intersection. Wearing stilettos and a flaming red dress, she fell near the corner, her dress opening like a wildflower and her legs splayed, revealing red panties.

Julián uttered, *"Cura! Cura!"* a calo term for "Watch out! Guys!"

The boys all turned around and sneaked a peek at her undies. They caught sight of the red material folded inward, revealing a deep slash. Right here, Julián hissed, "Juicy fruit!" Brother Hector looked at Max instead of Julián.

"What did you say?"

Max looked stunned and shrugged. Brother Hector assumed Max had said something inappropriate. As the boys marched single-file to the rectory, Brother Hector grabbed Max by the collar and asked him, "I heard you say something nasty. Now, what did you say?"

"I didn't utter a word," Max said.

"You're a liar! A bald-faced little liar!" Brother Hector slapped him across the face. The slap was so hard it practically knocked him down. Julián rushed to his friend and kicked the brother in the ass, making him tip over his Cossack habit landing on the ground. Julián was not about to let his friend take the blame.

Red-faced, Brother Hector seized them by the ears and hurried them to the rectory office, where Father Parks had witnessed the entire episode. He took hold of a longboard next to his writing desk, while Father Parks stood outside with a paddle in hand.

"You don't have to tell me anything. I saw the whole thing," he said.

"That's just the tip of the iceberg," Brother Hector added.

"Ohh, so there's more!"

At that point, the brother told him about the fallen prostitute, the red panties, and the "juicy fruit" commentary. Julian recalled the incident but embellished it with a fantasy ending. Max knew that wasn't how it'd happened, but he let Julian exaggerate, since he'd probably include it in the Fray Don Jose story.

"So, what's your pen name? Because I know you aren't using your real name?" Max asked.

"Hector Parks"

"*Qué cabron*," Max laughed.

"It still needs a good ending, Julián."

"I'm having Princess Morning Sun get her revenge. They are going to accost the soldiers and castrate them," Julián added.

"Not realistic, my friend."

"Why not?"

"Soldiers would arrive and decimate the Indian village, including Chief Soaring Eagle and the Morning Sun."

"So, what's your idea of an ending?"

"Why don't you have the Princess give birth to a mixed baby? Have him grow up and kill the mother's rapists."

Julian thought it was a ridiculous ending, and no one would believe it.

"I'll think about it."

* * *

THAT NIGHT, Julián headed off to his midnight shift, preoccupied with his story and contemplating what to do about his characters, especially the Indian maiden and her Chieftain father. He had drawn inspiration from observing the late-night customers ordering breakfast and receiving complimentary coffee because they were senior citizens.

He even noticed a big-breasted woman with her teenage daughter sitting calmly by a window, loudly discussing their mounting bills.

The manager, a heavyset man named Cruz, and his assistant, Fred Aleman, watched the customers through the mounted cameras. Inside the office, they would look at the computer screen, zooming in across the area in search of big-breasted women. Aleman often asked Julián to persuade customers—

especially women—to sit closer to the mounted cameras while he mopped the floor, as the camera with better reception was positioned there. Julián hated all these antics.

That evening, a hostile customer entered the restaurant looking for Cruz and Aleman. He claimed that one of them had made vulgar remarks about his daughter. He overheard them while waiting in the cab, as his wife and daughter ate in the restaurant. Disliking fast food, he remained in the truck until they finished their early breakfast. The husband noticed the heavy-set Cruz laughing, grabbing his crotch, talking on his cell phone, and making lewd comments about his wife and daughter. Aleman went outside to talk to Cruz, and both were laughing and watching videos on a cellphone. Aleman had uploaded close-ups of cleavage and breasts. They both went through the counter and into an office. The man had witnessed everything. He was not going to let it go without a fight.

The upset husband walked in, pounded the counter, and asked for the manager. His wife and daughter got up, startled at the commotion.

"*Qué pasa, hombre?*" his wife asked.

"Nothing," the husband said. "We need to leave."

The daughter was about thirteen, wearing a halter top and shorts, while the wife, a busty woman of forty, strikingly resembled the daughter; both could be mistaken for sisters. Julián heard the commotion and couldn't help noticing a bulge in the father's rear pocket. It's probably a gun, he thought. The situation could get serious. Cruz stepped out with Aleman by his side.

"How can we help you?" Cruz asked.

"You can help me by apologizing to my wife and daughter. I heard you and that peep-squeak laughing lewdly and pointing at my daughter and wife while they were eating. I saw both of you looking at a phone video," the angry father said.

"I beg your pardon," Aleman chimed in.

They both had guilty faces. Cruz looked scared, and Aleman was defiant.

"We will do no such thing. I'll call the police if I must," Aleman said.

"Go ahead. They'll agree with me after I show them this cell video, I made of you guys laughing and making lewd gestures behind the store. I recorded the whole damn thing," the father said.

Of course, the father had done no such thing, but he might have recorded them. Aleman changed his tone while Cruz got nervous.

"Let's talk about it privately, sir."

It was three in the morning when Julián stopped mopping and turned to Aleman, gesturing with his hand like a gun. He was trying to indicate to Aleman that the man had a gun. The whole situation felt like a bad dream, and people were bound to get hurt, as they often do in most shootings. Aleman and Guzman stepped out from behind the counter and calmly reasoned with the man while his wife and daughter stood behind him.

"Look, whatever you think happened didn't happen," Cruz said. Aleman was reaching for something under the counter.

"Don't move, mister, or I'll blast your face off," the man shouted, brandishing his .38 revolver.

Aleman was trying to close the register drawer, thinking it might be a holdup.

Customers scattered. Julián looked amazed, thinking this could serve as inspiration for his story. Stupid Cruz and his sidekick Aleman were staring down the barrel of a .38 Special. It didn't get any better than this. The father pistol-whipped Cruz while his wife poured hot coffee over Aleman. It was over in seconds.

They dashed out and sped away in a late-model truck. When police arrived, they wanted to know if anything had been stolen. Nothing. The next day, a detective asked if the inside cameras had recorded anything. Aleman and Cruz looked at each other and said the cameras had been inoperable. They lied, of course.

When Julián got home, Teresa asked if anything exciting had happened at work.

"Nothing. Just the same old, same old."

After eating breakfast, taking a dump, and showering, Julián retreated to his room and began typing where he had left off.

———————

ONE DAY, Princess Morning Sun, Chief Soaring Eagle, and his braves waited for Corporal Cruz and Aleman to mount up and search for game. Winter would soon be upon them, and Spanish provisions were months away. Deer, fish, and wild turkeys were plentiful. When the pair dismounted, Chief Soaring Eagle signaled his braves, and the screaming Apaches descended with tomahawks in hand and arrows aimed at them.

"Now, you talk. Confess to your white Father in the sky." Princess Morning Sun barked.

Both Aleman and Cruz were shocked, kneeling before a panel of warriors.

Princess Morning Sun dismounted.

She approached them and said, "Pray for a quick and merciful death."

She held a sharp, obsidian knife. Aleman and Cruz closed their eyes, weeping and praying louder, confessing their sins, admitting guilt, and asking for forgiveness. The braves covered the soldiers' eyes with vellum cloths and again urged them to confess to taking advantage of Princess Morning Sun. Unknown to Cruz and Aleman, Fray Don Jose and Commander

Captain Esteban Acosta had been eyewitnesses who had heard enough and ordered the men arrested. The captain and Fray Don Jose had been hidden in the bushes and trees, listening to all the confessions. Before the incident, Chief Soaring Eagle and Princess Morning Sun had informed Commander Acosta about what had transpired. Acosta explained that he needed proof because natives had no jurisdiction over Spanish soldiers, especially since their King and the Holy Church protected them. In short, they required proof and evidence from the commander, as their laws dictated.

"What is this proof?" Chief Soaring Eagle asked.

"A confession of the dirty deed."

"You shall get it!" Princess Morning Sun responded.

"But wait. We must be there as witnesses."

And it was decided that Princess Morning Sun would get her chance to prove beyond a doubt that she had been abused, and justice needed to be meted out. When Chief Soaring Eagle asked Morning Sun if she was satisfied, she said yes. The men were placed in leg irons, and Cruz was stripped of his rank.

Commander Acosta retold the incident involving Chief Soaring Eagle and Morning Sun as he took time during the early morning reflections and announcements to remind his soldiers that sins against the flesh were punishable by the Spanish Crown and would not be tolerated. Chief Soaring Eagle and Morning Sun left the Mission satisfied with the outcome. Fray Don Jose continued his duties, hearing confessions, tending the garden, and converting the Indians to the Catholic faith.

Later that night, the teenage Indian girl who cleaned the pisspots snuggled beside Fray Don Jose in his straw cot and pressed her breasts against his face. Don Jose blew out the candle and was thankful that Aleman and Cruz had been punished.

FRANKIE AND CARLY

Carly met Frankie at the Texas Theatre during the steamy summer of '68.

It was a hangout for teens. She was there with her cousin Cassie, decked out in grungy bell-bottoms and yellow eyeshadow, making her eyes pop like wild sunflowers. They both wore stringy love beads and Peace-Sign earrings. At the concession counter was this guy named Frankie.

Frankie was waiting for a friend and kept looking at his watch. Cassie spotted Frankie first and then pointed him out to Carly. Frankie had just turned 16 and was wearing battered jeans, a blue tee with gray shark fins, and dark aviator glasses. The kids all dressed the same because it was the sign of the times. He turned to look at Carly, ignoring Cassie. Carly's flashy eyes, snug-fitting blouse, and busty shape drew his attention. In the end, it was her giggly demeanor and captivating smile that won his heart. And to top it off, she had the whitest straight teeth he'd ever seen.

Frankie looked at his watch one last time and figured his blind date wasn't showing up, and this girl was just as good as the one he was waiting for. They talked briefly at the candy counter and became instant friends. Carly thought Frankie was a dreamboat. This wasn't good news for Cassie, who believed she had first dibs on Frankie, even though he never acknowledged her. A scent of patchouli and Taboo, famous at the time, wafted in the air. And Carly looked precisely like the fashion model Twiggy, whose face was plastered on Vogue and Teen mags at the time.

Fidgety, licking her lips and fixing her hair, Carly looked like every teenager's dream while her chubby cousin Cassie, was constantly dieting and wearing tighter clothes making her boobs pop out like pink balloons. Older guys often gravitated to Cassie first, but then shifted to Carly, whose heavy makeup made her look older.

"Let's hang out, okay!" Frankie said.

"Sure, you're on."

They maneuvered their way to the balcony to watch "Godzilla." The Saturday matinee was packed with young, tightly embraced couples and rows of kids, all clutching tubs of buttered popcorn and sweaty paper cups of Coke. The lights dimmed, and the show started. They sat near a corner aisle, snuggling while Frankie wrapped his arm around Carly. Poor Cassie sat two rows behind, sulking, slurping a blue Icee, and eating cheesy nachos.

Feeling sad for Cassie, Carly stole a glance at Cassie, who gave her a pissed off glance. She knew Cassie only hung around her to get guys, too. After the show, Frankie walked Carly to the corner of Coney Island Weiner Place on Houston Street. The sulky Cassie tagged behind them, putting on a brave front. If he only knew the truth, she thought. Before she could say anything, Carly gave Frankie her phone number, and Frankie gave Carly hers. After waiting a long while at the corner, the girls boarded the No. 41 bus line.

They ambled to the rear; Cassie was tight-lipped as they went home. When Carly opened her purse, Cassie stole a glance at the yellow slip and memorized Frankie's phone and address, pretending nothing unusual had happened. For them, it was just a regular Saturday.

* * *

AT HOME, Cassie debated whether to call Frankie or go to his house that night. She decided right then to go to Frankie's house to tell him the truth about Carly. The boy lived four blocks away from Cassie in a two-story tenement with his grandparents and mother. While she walked to her destination, Cassie hesitated about whether to return or proceed with the plan. Too late, she was there at his doorstep. She rang the doorbell and heard a woman shouting, "Don't ring the goddam buzzer! The baby's asleep!"

A short while later, she heard footsteps scrambling down the stairs. Frankie opened the door. He was surprised to find Cassie, not Carly.

"Hey, what's up? Where's Carly?"

"I'm sorry if I woke everybody up."

"Aww, don't worry. Where's Carly?"

"That's why I'm here," Cassie said.

She sprang into action, and she spewed out the venom: "You know, she's only twelve." Frankie's face turned white, and she looked perturbed.

"What the...?" Frankie said.

There was a long pause as if Frankie was sizing her up and searching for words to respond, as Cassie stared at him and added, "That's right. Jailbait—just twelve-years-old." She could see Frankie pondering, getting angry as he suddenly stepped out from inside and shut the door quickly. The neighborhood was abuzz with the usual kids on skateboards doing fancy sidewalk flips, and the neighbor across the street was mowing the lawn.

Cassie folded her arms, grinning sarcastically, studying his reaction as Frankie was sizing up the situation, trying to figure her motive: was it true or some ruse to test him? Frankie's brain was processing it all, but the word "jailbait" hung like a death sentence. He struggled to maintain his cool, but remembered a boy named Fast Eddie being arrested for an underage relationship with a girl almost the same age as Carly. It didn't help that he had a shotgun wedding.

Frankie wasn't amused with the storyline and wouldn't take it without a fight.

"Whoa! Wait a minute. She told me she was fifteen, almost sixteen," Frankie uttered, shaking his head.

"That's a lie," Cassie said, grinning.

She bit her lip, suggesting other intentions. But Frankie wasn't buying it. Just then, Cassie inched closer, pulling on his belt loops toward her. She had a wicked smile.

"Whoa there, Annie Oakley!" He pulled her hands off.

Embarrassed, she said coyly, "I wanted to tell you, but we never got a chance to talk."

Frankie took a defensive step back, letting everything come out. This wasn't going down as she had planned, and Cassie was reconfiguring the story, even if it was slightly off. Something about it didn't seem right to Frankie. And just as he was about to question her motives, Cassie blurted, "You know it's not right."

Frankie stayed quiet, allowing her to expand on her motive, looking straight into her eyes. Cassie pursed her lips, thinking Frankie should be grateful for saving his hide. Instead, Frankie reacted, "Yeah, you're right. I'm gonna call her and get to the bottom of this!"

Cassie hadn't expected this. He stepped inside and slammed the door on her face. Standing there looking stupid, Cassie's next step was to run to Carly and tell her the news. Everything was going to come out anyway.

Minutes later, Frankie phoned Carly. Angry. Confused. His

mind drifting—- She's a good kisser. No way, she's only twelve. After four rings, she answered the phone. In his mind, her voice even sounded younger. Frankie slammed her: "Carly, you lied to me. It's over. I don't ever want to, you see. Don't call me, okay!"

Carly's jaw dropped. "Frankie, what in the world are you saying?"

"You know? Don't give me that bull crap!"

"No, I don't."

"Don't be so stupid, Carly! You lied to me. Cassie told me everything!"

Click. The phone line went dead. Carly stared at the receiver, trying to understand just what had happened. She stifled her tears and hung the receiver back in its cradle. She knew something was wrong because her cousin Cassie said Frankie would find out about her sooner or later. She clenched her teeth and began sobbing. She grabbed her compact mirror. She looked at her face. She was a mess—like Alice Cooper with mascara-stained eyes.

Why does Cassie always do this? Carly rushed to the bathroom, washed her face, and applied a fresh coat of makeup. She did a quick lip job and slapped on fake eyelashes. She rushed downstairs and skipped breakfast. Her mom was standing at the stove, flipping hotcakes as she ran downstairs. Her mother turned around and saw her, saying, "Where in God's name are you going dressed like that?"

"Gotta go, mom! Cassie needs me!"

"Why are you dressed like that?"

"Sorry! Love you!"

She slammed the door and rushed to catch a city bus to Frankie's house.

Along the way, Carly thought about what Frankie knew and what Cassie had told him about her. She did lie about her age, as she was closer to thirteen in a few months. More lies. She was in a jam. That stupid Cassie, she thought, as more lies were piling up.

She tugged at the get-out bus wire, hopped off, and dashed to the Alazan housing projects. Young men standing on street corners wolf-whistled her. They laughed when she flipped them and went about their business. She turned the corner on El Paso Street, and the only two-story tenement was within reach.

She rang the buzzer. She heard someone coming downstairs, and the door opened. A girl wearing a towel on her head opened. "What do you want?"

"I need to talk to Frankie."

"He ain't here."

"I just finished talking to him."

"Well, you just missed him."

From the side, Frankie suddenly appeared. His sister scowled at him, saying, "Next time, don't ask me to lie for you, Frankie." When his sister left, Frankie stepped closer to the door, looking her up and down. He wondered how she'd manage to look older beyond her years.

"You sure fooled me. I was a sucker, wasn't I"?

"No, please. Please stop it. It wasn't like that."

"What was it? A cruel joke? Is that what you and your cousin do—play funny games?"

Carly could feel her heart pounding. She had to think fast. She buried her face in her palms and began sobbing. She inched closer to Frankie, thinking he was the best thing that ever happened to her. She reached out to put her arms around him. But Frankie rebuffed her, stiffening his arms at his side. He won't even hold me, she thought. I've lost him.

"Goodbye, Carly! It's over!" Frankie turned around and slammed the door. He hated being so cold-blooded, but he wasn't going to be the butt of any joke. Carly stood there, thinking, This is it. It's over. She stared at the door, debating whether to ring the buzzer again. But it was useless. The charade was over. She walked away, even considering going to a priest—crazy thoughts racing through her mind. From afar, Frankie peeked through the curtains. He watched from above, thinking, maybe in another three years—fat chance. A flashback of Fast Eddie and his arrest for the underage teen snapped him back to reality.

* * *

WHEN CARLY GOT HOME, her mother said Cassie had called. She said nothing and rushed upstairs to her room. She knew Cassie wanted to discuss what had happened with Frankie and explain her actions.

"Clean up your room! It's a mess," her mom yelled as she left for work. A stack of laundry awaited her. She was taking off her makeup when the doorbell rang. She went downstairs and opened the door. Before she could say a word, Cassie blurted: "Don't be pissed off!"

"Why did you tell him, Cassie? Why? I was going to tell him everything."

"I just told him you were underage. I kept the secret!"

"It's not right," Cassie said.

"I was going to tell him, anyway!"

"It wouldn't have lasted. He would have found out."

Carly looked at the mirror with Cassie by her side and saw peach fuzz growing on her chin. Cassie went to the closet, threw her a pair of denim jeans and a boy's shirt, and tossed them at Carly.

"For God's sake, be yourself! I kept your secret—-Carlos," Cassie added.

SHORT LIFE

*G*ermán Guerrero woke up from a bad dream.

He had been thinking of *El Memo*, his archenemy, and a day had not passed without seeing the foul face of Artemio Cruz, aka El Memo. Sending a message that would incite him to violence was necessary for his removal. He looked around, searching for anyone expendable. He found Ramon fretting with his cell phone and targeted him immediately.

"Tell Memo I'm gonna bust his snout!"

Ramon stopped what he was doing, looking confused, wondering if the message was meant for him. Ramon's simple English was basic, and Germán was aware of it. The rest of the Eighteenth Street gang scattered quickly, knowing Germán was in a bad mood. His anger was incredibly frightening because he could come up with worse things just for fun. They were all prisoners of circumstance, so vast yet so narrow, so suffocatingly filled with hot air.

"*¿ Qué, Qué?*" Ramon asked, puzzled.

"Clean your ears, *ese.*"

Germán was itching for a fight because Los Rowdies (Memo's gang) had intruded onto Eighteenth Street boundaries.

Ramon listened carefully and thumbed the phrase "Gonna bust his snout" into his translator app, and the words *le voy a romper el hocico* popped up. The word snout was not as horrific as hocico. But he shook his head because delivering that message would no doubt kill the messenger.

Ramon was a quick learner. He had been in the States for six months, traveling with a Coyote from Juarez, zigzagging road-blocks and dodging the clever migra. He found pochos, a strange species because they fought over a crappy piece of American leftovers. He felt it was all counterproductive. But Ramon agreed to deliver the message because he also belonged to the Nineteenth Street vatos, who lived in poorer, ragged tenements. Still, it was all beside the point because Ramon had been thinking of Betty, a Chola from California who had just moved into the hood.

Germán grinned at the pendejo and repeated, "Tell him I'm gonna bust his damn snout." The translator app repeated the simple command: *"Dile que le voy a reventar su pinche Hocico!"*

He grinned at the silly message and shook his head.

Germán added, *"Aprende Ingles, pendejo!"*

"I will, *ese.*"

Nineteenth Street gangsters weaponized the English language against the newest arrivals. They used couriers to travel between gangs from the West and East Coasts, delivering cryptic Spanglish messages back and forth through forbidden territories. He obeyed his American jefe, Germán Guerrero, the square-jawed, high-cheekbone guy with muddy eyes and a slight lisp who ruled with an iron fist. Germán was also from the same Juarez neighborhood as Ramon, which is why he joined the crew without the formal, ritualized beating. The passing months made American English easier for Ramon because he listened to the sing-song rhythms and double enten-dres of English, which were translated into Spanish, helping him understand why English was a harsher, coarser language.

Even his diction became more nuanced because gringos never revealed their true intentions, and business was numero uno. All his cholo friends listened to gangster rap, watched every episode of *Breaking Bad*, and followed the ruling clan of *Game of Thrones*.

Waves of new immigrants arrived in El Barrio, crowding gunshot shanties lining alleyways and vacant houses without running water or indoor privies. Even rats coexisted with them, finding any nook and cranny to etch out a living. They all competed for the cramped territory their ancestors had relinquished, making a small patch of dirt their home. Knowing who was a friend or a potential enemy was harder every day. At home, Ramon saw his parents laboring at two or three jobs, cleaning houses, mowing lawns, always one step ahead of bill collectors and the migra—those damned green monsters, those exterminators of dreams. His siblings, all girls, were expected to help, even the youngest one, Sara, who was barely four years old. His father, Jesús, had rebuked Ramon to the point of kicking him out ("I didn't ask to be born, you know!"), for disrespecting him. He walked down cobbled streets and dirt alleyways. His appearance made older women clutch their children, fearful of his neckline tats, military crewcut, and long sleeves worn in winter and summer.

When Ramon turned the corner of Guadalupe St. and 19th —the demarcation line between rival gangs —he found *El Memo* —the squat, stocky Artemio Cruz with rodent-like, dark eyes and predatory white teeth—sitting on his haunches with his homies, smoking mota. Just looking at him gave him the heebie-jeebies. Delivering the threatening message was the last thing on his mind. There was something creepy about *El Memo*—even his nickname stuck like chicle to the roof of his mouth. The night before, *El Memo*'s face had given him night sweats. He dreamed the smiling *Memo* laughing like *La Santa Muerte*, wagging its bony finger, warning him to stay away from

Germán and their neighborhood gang. He shook off the repellent dream, telling himself it was a dream. Those unsettling dreams made Ramon yearn for a better life, something greater than himself.

In his mind, the message from Germán was a scrambled jigsaw puzzle, and Ramon knew *El Memo* was nothing but a squatting *pendejo* taking a shit. He caught the eye of one of Memo's punks, who pointed his index finger at him. They had been waiting for a marked courier.

"*Chapete*, come over here!" The monkey face punk commanded.

He grinned and repeated his demand, "*Oye guey, Chapete!*"

Ramon hated the word *Chapete*. Another machismo stance signifying nothing. No way, Jose, he thought.

Another lieutenant mumbled, "State your business, ese." He knew it was all ritualized bravado played with malice and impunity.

Suddenly, *El Memo* snapped his fingers, and the punks stopped their menacing interrogations.

"*Que pasa, carnalito?* What's your Jefe's message?"

Before Ramon could utter the "shut your damned snout" insult, other words involuntarily leaped out: "Germán wants a peace treaty, bury the hatchet, like the great chiefs used to do."

There was a long pause before the punks laughed and slapped their thighs with a hilarity reserved for a George Lopez sitcom. *El Memo* didn't laugh. He peered straight at Ramon, determining his veracity like a brujo interpreting an egg yolk in a glass of water with all its stringy, bloody veins. *Memo* got so close to Ramon that he could smell his garlicky breath and flickered, "*Por qué?* Tell me why, *ese?*"

Another long pause. He could see his shark eyes because *El Memo* knew bloodshed was bad for business. He knew this because of *The Godfather* movies, where mafiosos governed with intellect and business acumen.

He knew *El Memo* wanted to be a businessman, to build an American empire, to consolidate, and to network with other gangs to create *"Puentes de Fe"* ("Bridges of Faith"), with a drug pipeline that flowed uninterrupted like El Chapo's underground tunnels. But he also knew they were all in the cesspool together.

"I'm waiting, ese," *El Memo* retorted.

Monkey-face grew angry at the disrespectful tone because Ramon was not even a ranking member of Nineteenth Street.

But Memo snapped his fingers, and all posturing stopped. The bulging, muscular Ramon grinned and replied, "Because it's good for business. *Ese!*" The Rowdies were trying to decipher what was going down, and then *El Memo* laughed wickedly, revealing his impeccably white teeth that gleamed and glistened. *"Tas cabron*, you hit the bull's eye, ese!"

The fates had intervened, and Ramon extracted a promise to arrange a Great Gathering between the two rival gangs. When he returned to his territory, Ramon convinced Germán that *El Memo* wanted a Peace Treaty despite his *hocico* reference, even giving him the lion's share of the profits. Germán stayed quiet, mulling it over, and consulted los brujos, the sorcerers who summon voices from the other side, who saw all and knew all. Even *la Santa Muerte* ruled the Aztec Empire before the coming of Quetzalcoatl and Hernán Cortés.

All the gangs competed with one another for shipping routes and insurance rackets. They extorted money from mom-and-pop stores that sought protection from accidental fires, property loss, and petty theft. Germán knew Nineteenth Street gangs excelled at offering security services despite being the ones who stirred up all the trouble. Ramón mused, wondering what invisible force compelled him to propose such a ridiculous agreement. He contemplated, searching for meaning in a nonsensical situation until a lightbulb flickered in his mind. Of course, it was that Betty girl who captured his heart. The raven-haired sixteen-year-old who was nobody's lackey: the free-thinking Califas chola who stood apart from her peers. Raised by her father, a middleweight prizefighter who died from a lethal blow, she now lived with relatives. He had investigated her background because he wanted to make a move. Betty Fuentes had grand dreams of status and power, projecting a force of nature that defied her gender. She had turned down Germán's and Memo's advances despite tacky gifts, offers of Gucci clothes, dozens of thorny roses, and even filthy threats.

"Hey, baby doll. Why don't I show you a good time?" *El Memo* wooed her. But Betty had retorted, "I'm not your baby, much less your doll. Step away *pendejo*! Before I bash your teeth. Move it," They all laughed at her huevos ("She's got balls of steel, more *huevos* than *los pendejos del barrio*"). Los Rowdies were shocked. Memo was dazed, his mouth agape.

The same happened to Germán and the Nineteenth Street homies who courted her. They gave up and began spreading chisme about her. "She's a dyke, a man-flora," Germán scowled.

A late-August arrangement was made for the Great Gathering between Germán and *El Memo*. But Ramon was focused on Betty, trying to figure out a way to win her over. They'd bump between classes at school and exchange greetings— nothing serious. Even though Ramon didn't attend school, he roamed the hallways during classes and hung out after school because he knew she lived a few blocks away. He ate at Speedy's Fried Chicken place, a student hangout during lunchtime. He went there and stared at her. Something about Ramon drew her, and Betty saw some potential in him. If only he'd cleaned up his act, she thought, removed the tats, and dressed differently, the young man would be attractive, good-looking, and, perhaps, a good catch.

"Are you following me or what?" She stared at Ramon, who smiled and lowered his eyes, embarrassed.

She was too pretty for him, he thought. But Betty was careful not to appear too firm, so she smiled at him before she turned away. She had thrown him a line and hoped he'd take the bait.

One day, Betty was laying flowers at her father's grave, something she did every Sunday. She had forgotten it was Mother's Day, and she saw Ramon kneeling at a grave when he solemnly kissed a granite tombstone. Touched by his tenderness, Betty was moved by that solemn act and remembered her father's comment ("A man is not afraid to show his feelings, not afraid to cry"). Ramon was built like her dad, hefty and naturally muscular. The San Fernando Cemetery was filled with flowers and bouquets as Mother's Day was a national holiday. Everything stopped. Feuds were temporarily forgotten. Any sign of disrespect was ignored or put aside until another time.

She sauntered quietly behind him. "Was she your mother?"

A little taken aback, Roman turned around, embarrassed.

"I'm sorry. I didn't mean to startle you," Betty said. Her soft, soothing voice, ebony eyes, and fleshy lips mesmerized him. She had a gentle side despite all the nasty lies spread about her. She wore a beautiful black dress that clung to her skin yet was tasteful, not coarse like the hootchie-chickas of Los Rowdies.

"It's okay; you didn't. It's my abuela. I miss her so much."

Betty offered flowers to him. "I had these extra roses. I thought you might like them for your loved one."

His abuela had a special place in Ramon's heart because she taught him that God had other great things in store for him. Ramon's eyes got watery when he thought about his Abuela Petra and how much she prayed for God's intervention. He wondered about Betty because all this had come as a surprise. He had prepared scenarios and mental episodes on approaching Betty, but Ramon hadn't expected a chance to meet at a cemetery.

"I'm so sorry. I know how you feel," Betty added, touching his shoulder.

He felt a strange connection, reflexively drawing closer to

her. They gave each other obligatory hugs reserved for kindness and respect. But somehow, this felt different. They sensed fate tethering them together like a cosmic vein connecting her heart to his heart, his soul to her soul. She sighed heavily, and the hug lasted longer than expected. Then the inevitable happened: Ramon kissed her lips. She didn't recoil; instead, she touched his face gently and smiled. Slowly, Betty withdrew, shamefully thinking that the place and time were inappropriate for the occasion, even tempting fate.

"I'm sorry. I don't know what got into me," Ramon apologized. "Don't worry," she smiled. "Maybe it was meant to happen."

They met again at Speedy's Chicken Place. Before long, Betty and Ramon became inseparable, and rival gangs didn't care either way because somebody was bound to hook up with her. The more Betty and Ramon were together, the more Ramon felt the pull of fatherhood. He wasn't cut out for this gangland business. Raising a family this way was counterproductive, and Betty told Ramon the gangland stuff limited his opportunities.

"You want something better than this?" Betty told him.

"Like what?"

"Start your business—I don't know."

"Maybe," Betty paused and uttered, "Finish your education!"

Ramon thought long and hard. Of course, that was a good two years away. He loved negotiating with people. A teacher once told him he was a natural with numbers; a friend even advised him to get his G.E.D.

Betty agreed to help him accelerate his success quickly. He signed up for special classes, paid his initial fees, and took the high school equivalency exam. A month later, Ramon got the results and a certificate. He was set.

A community activist reached out to him about a City Gang Specialist Liaison position in the Youth Intervention Program.

But Ramon flatly turned it down. He had other plans. He was seen leaving a downtown attorney's office. Nineteenth Street vatos weren't happy. Even Germán felt betrayed because he'd fallen for Betty's talk about finding something better than what his homeboys had to offer.

With August looming closer, the Powwow was approaching between Nineteenth Street and Los Rowdies. Ramon was suddenly forbidden to attend; he had been tagged a civilian, unworthy of inclusion, and even told not to wear their colors. Betty told him it was for the better. Ramon and Germán were heading for a separation.

"You're out, dude, not even a member," Germán snarled. "Nobody wants you."

Ramon and Betty were seen as two star-struck lovers who didn't know whether they were coming or going.

Ramon retorted, "Don't need anybody, *carnal.*"

"You ain't my *carnal.*" Germán spat to the side in disgust and walked away with his entourage.

And all this time, Ramon thought he was moving up. It was time to part ways, and the act of separation was truly brutal, a savage blow worse than the first. But Germán offered him a solution, a painless way to split. There was no fight or Hollywood-style drama—just a simple, you're nothing-but-shit to us. Betty and Ramon celebrated that evening, relieved because they would soon be married. Everything felt like a dream come true. A happy Betty, turning seventeen, and Ramon was becoming her real man.

At dusk, a dark Chevy Malibu cruised and parked outside. Ramon peeked through the curtains. It was hard to identify those inside because the windows were black. He had never seen that car in the neighborhood before.

"Please, Ramon. It's a trap," Betty begged.

"Don't worry. They got nothing on me." He stepped out of the screen door and walked to the passenger side.

The dark glass rolled down. "*Ese,* Ramon. *Soy yo, Flaco.* Memo's cousin from Califas." The depraved Flaco was a menace with skull tattoos over his face and fiery red demons down his neckline. He flashed his gang sign—the guys in the rear seat wore black and gray colors with checkered bandanas—and even the driver looked demonic.

"*Qué ondas.* What's up?"

"Heard you ain't with Germán no more. Just one last favor, *Carnal.*"

"I'm listening, *ese.*"

A cholo in the rear lifted a thick, aluminum briefcase, flipped the latches parallel, and opened it with a key. Inside were Franklins neatly stacked. Flaco had been out of prison a month and was already a significant player.

"It's a token to Germán from the brotherhood," Flaco smirked. His rodent eyes looked lifeless. Ideas raced through Ramon, and he wondered if it was some trap.

"Why me, *ese?* I'm not a member anymore. You give it to him."

"*Orale. El Memo* knows about it, and we figured it's your last duty for the homeys. One last time, ese."

He bit his underlip, and, against his better judgment, Ramon said, "All right, I'll just give it to them, and then I'm out —okay?"

"That's all, *carnalito.*"

Before they handed him the heavy briefcase, the cholo flipped the latches sideways and locked it securely, and gave him the suitcase.

"The key, carnal?" Ramon asked.

"Don't worry," Flaco grinned. "We'll give Memo the key. He will open the briefcase."

Ramon lifted the heavy suitcase and placed it on the sidewalk. He walked inside with it, and the Malibu rumbled off, the radio blasting, "Cisco Kid." Betty came out and asked what they wanted. They hugged, and Ramon told her it was the last item on the check-off list.

"Deliver this suitcase to the meeting, and it's done. I'm out."

"What's in it?"

"A bunch of Franklins on one side and Grants on the other," Ramon said. Betty shakes her head, thinking, I'm teaching him slang well.

"You bugger you," Betty laughed, punching him on his shoulder. She hugged him and said, "*Te quero, mi amor*. I've been praying for this." The Great Gathering between Nineteenth Street and Los Rowdies occurred at midnight in a vacant house behind Alazan Apache homes next to a basketball courtyard. It was perfect. Isolated. Old cars line the streets. The neighborhood was eerily quiet; gangs sat around taking tequila shots, clinking Tecate bottles, and munching pizza.

Ramon entered with a suitcase in hand. Germán grinned sarcastically while *Memo* sat stone-faced, puzzled about Flaco's lavish gift. Ramon didn't want anything to do with exchanging goods, especially the twenty thousand, as a gift for burying the hatchet. Ramon placed the heavy suitcase on the table. He was about to walk away.

"*Orale*, Ramon. Let's see what you have. Open it," *Memo* uttered.

He gave Ramon the unique key. The boys gathered around the table, surrounded by gang members, because a peace treaty was about to be secured. *El Memo* was giving the first month's profits to the rival gang as an offering. They would seal the deal afterward with more boozing, sizzling fajitas, and snorting a couple of lines against the background noise of *War* and *Los Lobos*. Ramon inserted the key and snapped the latches. The briefcase opens.

A flash of light. A rumbling, thundering earthquake. Betty heard a loud explosion shattering windows in the vicinity, followed by the sound of ambulance sirens. Honking fire trucks barreled down Commerce Street. Barrio dogs howled. A cold chill embraced Betty. She then heard the rumbling muffler of a black Malibu drive past her house, blasting lowrider music. And right then, quite supernaturally, she heard Ramon's voice—*Te quero mi amor.*

The words echoed in her ear because Betty was carrying his child, unaware of Ramon's presence. Poor Ramon, they would have celebrated that evening, and then she would have shared the good news with him. She got up, ran to the bedroom dresser, lifted a large envelope, and opened it. Ramon had left recorded tapes of the gang's dealings, complete with listings of their assets, affiliate networks, addresses, contacts, and even Flaco's connections with the cartels, in case anything happened to him. Ramon also left an insurance policy. Betty knew what she had to do. She was carrying Little Ramon, who would live a better life than the short life of his father.

HOUSE OF THE DEAD

I'm outside, staring down at an ant colony. I drop a long, stringy gob into its opening. Bored, I wonder if ants feel the distant hum of the Earth's rotation. I have these strange ideas about nature's tiniest inhabitants and whether they have souls. The sky is cloudy. Thunder rumbles in the distance. The backyard oaks and hackberries stand quietly.

Like those ants, I imagine Mother Earth feeling the countless pricks of shovels as people bury their dead into her womb. These are turbulent times. Our Philco TV flashes black-and-white images of weary soldiers in Vietnam. Police brutalize Black civil rights protesters with water cannons and snarling dogs. The loud shot of Sirhan Sirhan killing Robert F. Kennedy at a hotel. Closer to home, Cesar Chavez advocates for migrant rights, boycotting grapes.

Everyone is suffering.

As a junior in high school, I wonder about my fate and destiny. Will I find a girlfriend for prom? What do my friends think of me? I stare at life's changes in the mirror, feeling as insecure as other teens. Time moves fast toward an unpredictable future. The weight of guilt and shame rolls into one cumulative ball—like a dung beetle rolling a shit ball up a hill. Sorrow. Grief. Pain. Regret. All the hollowness of despair is inching up from my belly, waiting to be released.

Just as I release another mighty gob of phlegm onto the ant pile, I see a shadowy man in a black suit approaching.

"They've been looking for you all day long. ¿On tavas? Where were you?" my uncle Antonio demands. He code-switches between English and Spanish, and the phrase "on tavas" is a rhythmic stab—a jab at my growing masculinity.

His tone is unapologetic, interrogatory, like a heavy anvil pressing against my chest. Those thirteen words burrow deep into my brain like slow-moving bullets shot from his accusatory finger. I must look like a fawn caught in a driver's headlights.

They've been looking for you all day long.

I resent his tone. He usually sees me as something lower than his servants, who help around the house. But this time feels different. His phrase carries concern. They were family members: cousins, my sisters, brothers, uncles—those clamoring for closure and those wanting the latest gossip.

¿On tavas? Where were you?

Two questions in two languages bordering the personal and objective, between Old World Spanish heritage and New World modernism. We use language in both intimate and public spaces: Spanish is closer to the heart, and English is more distant and less personal.

I was conspicuously absent from my grandfather's funeral. I violated cultural norms by not attending his services. In Uncle Antonio's eyes, I disrespected our Old Spanish heritage. But my neglect wasn't born of disrespect—it was painful trauma. I couldn't accept that my grandpa was gone. I couldn't bear to see him lying stiff in that coffin, eyes shut forever, with those creepy ceramic lamp-holding seraphim guarding his body.

Many people were there asking about my whereabouts. I

was condemned before I had a chance to prove my innocence, no doubt compared to my drunken father.

Most of all, I remember the days leading up to that fateful event.

I remember the shadowy evening we gathered around Grandpa as he lay delirious: "They're there. Strange shadows tell me to go with them, and I can't. I can't go. I have much to do."

I held him close, my hands on his face. "Grandpa, there's only us."

His pupils enlarged, then his forehead grew cold.

"They're here." He paused. "*Muchos niños*. Many children."

Grandpa said a ladder was suspended in mid-air with children around him, beckoning him to climb it. He had to climb the ladder; otherwise, the children would be mad at him.

A little later, Grandpa was dead.

Uncle Antonio arrived at that moment. He was the eldest— my father's only brother. Overweight, his dour features betrayed an unhappy childhood. His dark suits and matching black ties made his grey eyes shine like a menacing cat. It was customary for funeral directors to wear serious faces; it was part of the job.

"You've been disrespectful to *Abuelo Grande?*" His voice cut into me like a sharp blade.

Abuelo Grande—that's what he called my grandfather. I called him *mi Apa*, my father. He was more of a father to me than my birth father, who felt more like a sibling, a friend.

Grandpa raised me, protected me when my father came home drunk, wanting to whip me for no reason other than I was his favorite.

Uncle Antonio stared at me, then turned and walked away. Dismissive of my feelings without allowing me to explain. He was rebuking me for missing the funeral services. But he didn't understand—I couldn't say goodbye to a corpse when my grandfather wasn't dead but in heaven. In my mind, I refused to accept his death.

My grandma understood. She knew how much I loved and adored Grandpa, and she never scolded me for my wishes.

When I was a child, abuelo promised he'd never leave me. But on that fateful hour, we stood around his bedside asking God and the saints to intervene. We witnessed his last breath, trembling and uttering about strange shadows beckoning him to the other world.

My grandmother shouted: *"Dios mío*, they're coming for him. *Por favor, virginicita,* don't let them take him, please, I beg you." She prayed on her knees near her makeshift home altar of *La Virgen de Guadalupe*, asking Our Holy Mother to intervene and save her husband, who had been her partner for more than seventy years of marriage.

But he was gone. I touched his hand as it turned cold. Abuela covered his eyes, and he looked peaceful.

The ambulance arrived, and then the coroner verified his death. The man in a dark suit gave us condolences and said Grandpa had "passed on." The phrase lingered like foggy mist—his spirit traversing into an unseen world.

It was too much for me to think of Abuelo lying motionless, his body covered in a white shroud. Uncle Antonio stood there, eyes red, trying to mask his fragile feelings. I walked away to be alone in another room.

My father, Jose, wasn't there. Perhaps it was better since he'd break down sobbing. He probably felt shame and agony because he had never met my grandfather's expectations.

"Where's Jose?" Uncle Antonio asked my grandma.

"¿Quién sabe?" she said. Who knows.

I was within earshot and heard everything. Grandma always protected him, and Uncle Antonio was aware of it.

We lived on El Paso Street in a two-story stucco building. The first floor housed Uncle Antonio's funeral home office and chapel. The second floor was where my grandparents lived, and where I lived. The funeral home was the *Casa de Muertos*—the House of the Dead.

"Grandpa, I'm afraid of ghosts," I'd say.

He'd smile, put his arms around me. "Don't worry about the dead. It's the living you have to be afraid of."

And he was right. Every weekend, hordes of people gathered when funerals were staged on the first floor. Black-dressed ladies and men with dour faces made spectacles of themselves, flinging themselves around coffins as if they could raise the dead. I'd seen it all through a peephole that gave me a panorama of the whole ritual.

Sometimes fights broke out—sometimes a slighted relative, or perhaps one person owed money to the deceased. Often, drunken relatives spewed their guts about the departed as if the poor soul could respond to accusations. Uncle Antonio always placated them while the priest tried to calm them down.

The task of the funeral director was to calm relatives and relieve their suffering. Uncle Antonio was good at that. He truly cared about the deceased and their families, and I couldn't fault him for that. But understanding his dismissal of my grief—that was harder to forgive.

My grandma was another story. She always comforted Grandpa, gave him tobacco for his pipe, and rolled his Bugler-brand cigarettes. She was always doing things for him: making tea, and often, stealthily, stealing his hidden cash from a leather pouch under the mattress to give to Jose Chico for pocket money and his drinking habit. Abuelita was his enabler.

When Jose Chico tried to backhand us, Abuelo shielded us from his drunken rages. We'd huddle against him, and he'd rebuke his son: "*Sin vergüenza. Borracho. ¡Vámonos!*"

The rebuking words sent Jose Chico on his way to the cantinas. After a while, Grandpa would retrieve a mason jar filled with candies and give us sugared orange slices to help alleviate our sorrow.

Abuelita, however, always sided with Jose Chico. In her eyes, he could not harm her. He was the incarnation of the child with the same name she'd lost to the Influenza of 1919.

According to family history, my abuelita, Genoveva Ortiz, married Jose Castillo right after the Mexican Revolution of 1910. She'd crossed the Rio Grande as thousands had done to escape the bloody war. My great-great-grandfather, Francisco Castillo, once owned land in Mexico and businesses on the other side. When the Villistas confiscated their property and wealth, the only alternative was to flee Mexico and set up business on *El Otro Lado*—the other side.

The brothers had been rivals since birth. My grandpa favored Antonio, while Jose was my grandma's favorite. She pampered and protected him against the internal rages from my older, more successful uncle. Unlike the stereotypical Mexican abuelita, Genoveva was a diminutive woman who wore black, accompanied by a dark shawl that gave her an Eastern European appearance. Grandpa playfully called her *La Gachupina*—a Spaniard born in the New World.

Uncle Antonio had all the hallmarks of Spanish purity: a light complexion, light-colored eyes, and a bearing of superiority. My father was more mestizo—born of mixed blood, the result of a Spanish man mating with an Indian woman. Jose Chico was the title he bore because he was the junior in the family after my grandpa. He was my grandma's favorite because he'd chosen to stay with my grandparents, sheltered from hard work and responsibilities.

The family was broken because my father had made a mess of everything. When my parents separated—almost like divorce without the religious stigma—my brothers and sisters stayed with my mother, while my older sister Cecilia and I stayed with my grandparents. My oldest brother, Patricio, joined the military after a brief stint living with our cousins.

At the time of the funeral, I stayed away. It was better because I refused to see his body in the coffin. I wanted to remember him in my private way—Abuelo always comforting me when I feared *la Llorona* or when he saw me sad and playing by myself in a corner.

When all the people had left the cemetery, I said my good-byes to a mound of earth that covered my abuelo. But I refused to see my abuelito lying stiffly tucked inside that coffin. In my mind, my grandfather was not dead but in heaven.

Three years later...

I was seventeen and a senior at Sidney Lanier High School, a vocational training ground for future auto mechanics, body shop technicians, and the blue-collar lifestyle that would shape our futures. Ironically, the namesakes of both my schools were writers: James Fenimore Cooper (author of *The Last of the Mohicans*) and Sidney Lanier (a minor Confederate southern poet).

The school was located in the heart of the West Side. Our school's mascot was a metal screw nicknamed a Vok—short for vocational screw. The ironic symbol wasn't lost on bright-eyed students who read books for pleasure beyond rudimentary requirements. It was no mystery that we'd gotten screwed into dead-end jobs.

The city had always been divided: Latinos on the West Side, Blacks on the East Side. The prosperous North Side was reserved for upper-class whites and a handful of Latinos who owned businesses and identified as Spaniards. The South Side was relegated to poor whites.

After transferring from Cooper Junior High to Lanier High School, I remember my casual meeting with my high school counselor. Mrs. Smith was a blonde with a beehive hairdo, teardrop diamond-studded glasses, and piercing blue eyes. Her skin folded like a wrinkled turkey with gaudy jewelry adorning her neck.

"So, what do you want to do after high school?" she asked.

"I want to be a writer," I said.

She scribbled something on a yellow legal pad, then raised her eyebrow and lowered her lenses to the bridge of her nose.

"What is it you want to drive? Taxis or buses?"

She hadn't heard me, or perhaps misinterpreted my words.

I hesitated. "No. No. You don't understand. I want to be a story writer." I spoke clearly so she'd understand. The nuns at Guadalupe Catholic School had taught us proper pronunciation —they wanted us to learn quickly and eliminate the stigma of sounding like foreigners.

The old lady shook her beehive negatively, smiled politely, and stung me with her fountain pen, assigning me to the Commercial Art department.

"It's all we have, and I think Art is very close to writing— only with paint."

Like those ants I'd tormented, I was just another insignificant creature to be brushed aside, my dreams as easily crushed as an anthill under someone's heel.

Two years later...

When I was a junior, Lanier High School was going through changes. I was doing well in my journalism class, rising to the position of News Editor, while my friend Raymond Sanchez served as Sports Editor. But the real change was happening outside our classrooms.

Events were developing so quickly across America— protesters and walkouts in Chicago and Detroit, riots in Watts. The times were changing, as Bob Dylan sang. My friend Edgar Lozano was becoming increasingly radicalized, reading and watching as current events unfolded. I remember seeing Edgar sporting *"Chale Con El Draft"* and "Boycott Grapes" buttons on his shirt.

One afternoon, a month before our Ring Ceremony, Jostens's representative expressed regret that a backlog had occurred, and we might not have our senior rings ready for the March ceremony. Our senior sponsor, Mr. Whitcliffe, privately said that the company was not being forthcoming.

Suddenly, a hand lifted from the back row.

"I think it's a shame and cause for a lawsuit if the company cannot deliver what was promised in the contract." The student had the contract, read parts of it, and mentioned restitution and money-back guarantees. Soon, other hands went up, and the auditorium was in mayhem with shouting about the company's callousness.

Homer Garcia spoke eloquently about how Latino-dominated schools were always getting shafted because of our passivity. Homer was right. Our culture encouraged respect, honor, and humility as pillars of getting along in a civilized world.

A teacher barked, "Shut up and sit down! You're out of order!"

Homer Garcia was the apotheosis of Chicano consciousness growing during the radical 1960s. He read voraciously, became the intellectual defender of west-side politics, and was a great debater. I admired his bravado and the fact that he was risking himself for the benefit of our culture, our people.

La Raza—our people—was gaining momentum, a movement that began with Cesar Chavez's grape boycott. Our schools remained segregated despite President Johnson's passing of the Civil Rights Act of 1965. Some turncoat politicians claimed that Mexicans were white and shouldn't be grouped with African Americans. This hurt Mexicans because Texas courts maintained that San Antonio schools were compliant, which was a sham.

Soon, one of our local leaders—Sidney Lanier graduate Joe Bernal—became involved and began organizing community meetings at the Guadalupe Center, located behind Our Lady of Guadalupe Church. The "establishment" was the power structure that governed the economic engine, collected taxes, and supported segregated building codes that kept Chicanos en masse in barrios as easy workforce fodder.

My friends Steve Castro and Homer Garcia complained that Lanier didn't offer courses to enable us to pursue a university education. When we had student assemblies, the topics were usually pregnancy prevention for girls or dead-end jobs for boys. One day, we were assembled to hear four students talk about their harrowing experiences with drugs. Another time, ex-convicts and handcuffed prisoner trustees spoke about the dangers of gangs. It was all bizarre and condescending.

That was the defining moment when Steve and Homer decided to contact State Senator Joe Bernal. He agreed to meet with the Student Organization but asked them to bring their parents. "If you can get at least twenty parents," Bernal said, "I think we can make a case with the San Antonio School District Board."

The meeting surprised all of us. That evening, two hundred parents and community people packed the Guadalupe Church community center.

I sat in the back, thinking about Grandpa, how he'd always told me not to fear the dead but the living, how he'd protected me from my father's drunken rages, from Uncle Antonio's dismissive superiority, from a system that wanted to crush our dreams like ants under a heel.

But here we were—la raza—no longer scattered and isolated like those ants in my backyard. We were organizing, demanding better than the vocational screws they'd tried to turn us into. We were claiming our right to dream, to write our own stories, to climb ladders that weren't suspended in delirium but built with our own hands.

As Joe Bernal stood to address the crowd, I thought about

the strange shadows Grandpa had seen in his final moments. Maybe they weren't beckoning him to death but to this—to the moment when his grandson would understand that the real ghosts weren't the ones in the funeral home downstairs, but the living systems that tried to bury our hopes before we'd even had a chance to grow.

The revolution had just begun. And unlike those ants whose hills I'd thoughtlessly destroyed, we would rebuild—stronger, more united, impossible to ignore.

We were no longer scattered. We were home.

DIGITAL NATIVES IN THE CITY OF LIGHT

(To David Applefield)

They stood gazing at it, stunned. Manny and Freddy had traveled thousands of miles to cross the Seine River, and the bookshop looked tiny compared to what they'd seen in the picture ads. Hemingway had been there—so had Fitzgerald. The travel agency promoted the historic bookstore as a must-visit for anyone wanting to be a writer. But Freddy never aspired to be a writer. His father wanted to be one. He despised writers. Manny even told him that writers and bookstores were things of the past. Everyone has graphic novels, Manny was fond of saying to Freddy. But Freddy still believed books were essential items.

Manny added, "Writers are dope. You need to write code. Apps!"

Going to Paris was a graduation gift from their parents, both Gen Xers, who had made it big during the Dot-Com phase of the economy. Freddy's dad was a broker in Silicon Valley and a close friend of Manny's mom, who owned boutique shops around Berkeley. Both sets of parents were divorced in their minds, while their bodies remained married. That's what they'd learned from them—arranged marriages become open marriages.

They had gotten an apartment on the Left Bank and wanted to spend the day exploring the neighborhood on their skateboards. They had been considering doing things other than continuing their education.

"Freddy, did you tell your dad you're ditching Yale?"

Freddy smirked, saying, "I'll write him a check, and he'll be lit when I send him a stock option for a new app I've just created."

"Man. That's epic," Manny cracked, opening his MacBook. In cyber-reality, Freddy and Manny were hackers and app developers, making more "coins" than their parents combined. At eighteen, they didn't think college life would teach them anything they hadn't experienced in their lifetimes; they couldn't force themselves to devote four years of studying more Western nonsense when they were considerably greater stars than their buddies at Stanford.

"Hey, let's head down for some Soylent drinks and cheeseballs," Freddy quipped.

Manny nodded.

"We'll do that crusty bookstore junket and buy some postcards. So, my dad will know we spent time in that old dustbin."

Just as they were about to get their skateboards, the doorbell rang. Manny and Freddy looked at each other and wondered who it could be. Room service? No, impossible, thought Manny, not in these apartments. When Freddy opened the door, they discovered it was Miriam Heatherstone, their check-in mom, a grad student at the Sorbonne hired by Freddy's Dad to oversee their activities. Miriam was a blue-eyed blonde with skinny legs wearing Spandex and minimal makeup. She looked more Scandinavian than British.

"Hello, guys. Mind if I take you blokes to see the sights in the City of Lights?"

They stared at each other and then giggled at her unintentional rhymes.

"Yo, what lights? It's not even dark," Manny smirked. Miriam rolled her eyes and took a deep breath, thinking it would be a long day with these brats.

"I was hoping we would spend the day at the Louvre."

"The Louvre. That's so whack," Manny said.

They finally consented, but not without making snarky comments about museums and dead collectibles that were unworthy of their precious time. They both believed in soloing it and the pull of destiny, not the surreal moment when death and decay drag you to the center of non-action. They had internalized their parents' yoga philosophy, even though Freddy and Manny believed more in Yoda. They'd been friends since the early days of Coolio and Boyz II Men, born during the Columbine High carnage.

They wanted to explore Paris and hang out with cool people who never slept and always knew where to find the best stuff. They had laid out extensive plans after the trip. Freddy and Manny would move to the Big Apple and get a brownstone apartment in Hell's Kitchen. They were not geeks but nanotechs with a penchant for skateboards, Zanerobe pants, Yeezys, and Chipotle. After they ditched "Miriam the Stoner" because of her addiction to synthetic weed and because it contained no GMOs, the boys set out to the Left Bank, guiding past tour buses and long lines at the Louvre.

"What a fucking waste," uttered Freddy.

"For sure," Manny quipped.

They were inside the fabled Shakespeare and Company Bookstore in no time, paying homage as Freddy's father had suggested. It would be just another thing to check off on their list.

"Just crusty old books," Manny said.

"Yup, I don't know what the fuss is about."

"Hey, scope out if they have Game of Thrones," Freddy added.

To the boys, the place was just another nondescript bookstore set haphazardly, but it felt cozy to Grandpa there, unlike those drone-like corporate Barnes & Noble stores with nearby Starbucks. One day, a guy named Applefield was reading poetry from one of his many chapbooks. The boys looked at each other and smirked because the poetry scene was pretty lame and silly. Poetry was different from their cup of coffee. They did love graphic novels. Freddy had once told his dad that he wanted to be a graphic novelist and write about cool guys in flying carpets and giant dung beetles attacking New York City. His father said something about it being Kafkaesque, which Freddy misunderstood as "fuhgeddaboudit."

Both guys had grown up with cell phones and Mac Tablets. The world was their oyster. They were going to crack it open, with or without the pearl, as they guffawed and high-fived themselves. Then they noticed this girl about their age sitting quietly in one corner, reading intensely. Freddy smiled at Manny, smitten by the lonely damsel with red hair and dazzling blue eyes who exuded innocence. And it was Manny who intervened, asking in his demurred imitation of a cool Cole Sprouse or a younger Johnny Depp.

"Excuse me, but we were wondering if you're Canadian?"

The girl paused, placed the book down, and stared at the two boys. She smiled at Freddy, who looked like a younger version of Elijah Wood. And then, she turned to Manny and responded, "Nope, I'm American."

"I knew it," Freddy smiled. He made an air-high-five to Manny.

Manny had always been the one who received the second glance, the sidekick, like Tonto to the Lone Ranger, or the ugly one in Beavis and Butthead. Despite the Harambe Gorilla T-shirt with cherub wings and a halo, his body was lean and muscular. ("Take it off, Manuel. You look lame and ridiculous," his father had said.) Now, everything was coming into focus. The girl stared at his T-shirt.

"Ahhhh, poor thing. They should've spared him," she pouted.

And right there, Manny got strung. He felt the pull, and, for the first time, a tinge of jealousy aroused his better half. It had never happened before. Even at Berkeley High, the boys had never been crossed over a girl—not even that crazy Fernanda Wolf-Miller, who played them both for their calculus notes. It was bewildering that his heart succumbed to something Manny had never felt. Her name was Hadley, and she was an expat studying at the Sorbonne and majoring in literature.

"Could you join us for some coffee?" Freddy asked.

She stared at them both, smiled, and said, "How are you going to take me there? In your skateboards?" They all giggled. A patron let out a long shhh as if the old, stuffy, moldy bookstore had a spiritual connection to the Notre Dame Cathedral across the Seine. Luckily, Hadley had a Citroen parked nearby. They walked a few blocks with Hadley, skateboards in tow, hopped inside, and placed their boards in the back. Hadley Adams had been in France for three years and knew all the off-the-beaten-path places for desserts and fun. She enjoyed the nightlife and spent most of her time studying, writing papers, and conducting research. The bookstore was perfect for recharging, listening to Beat poetry, and relaxing with a good book.

"Don't you love books?" She smiled.

"Oh, yeah. Books are great," Manny uttered.

"Guys. So, what's on your reading list?"

Freddy was the first to say, "I love books; I just don't like them dominating my life." As if on cue, Manny responded, "Ohh, come on, Freddy. You love reading the first paragraph of a book and the last. That way, you can claim having read the book cover to cover."

Hadley laughed and thought it was hilarious. Freddy turned red, slightly shocked that Manny would turn on him.

Not to be outdone, Freddy retorted, "Hah, you should know. Your idea of a library is a collection of coloring books." More laughter and the boys' banter became sultry hot with Hadley as the object of their affection. The boys had never felt so engrossed before, and she was with them like a threesome forged from years of friendship. Freddy had read that Paris does that to people. Perhaps it was the air, or maybe something in the water. Whatever the case, Freddy and Manny had Hadley in stitches, laughing and giggling.

After a quick nightcap at Café de Flore on Boulevard Saint-Germain, Manny got a little bolder because he was more physically imposing than poor Freddy, who was indeed an intellectual with a seemingly tender demeanor. Without blinking an eye, Freddy asked Manny if they could talk privately in the bathroom.

"You're on," Manny said. They bought drinks and excused themselves. Hadley smiled, adjusted her earbuds, and plugged in music on her cell phone.

"Yo, my man, Three's a battalion. We've gotta split up," Manny said.

"That's right, dude. You are mucking it all up!"

"What? You wanna square up?"

"Hey, dude. I'm just going to yolo it. She's a fine specimen."

"That she is, my friend. I mean, we're connected," Freddy replied.

"So, let's have her decide," Manny insisted.

So, it was settled that they'd let Hadley be the judge. They returned to the sidewalk table and saw Hadley talking to a tall, slender guy with slick blonde hair who looked like a younger version of Leonardo DiCaprio. They walked to the table, and Hadley introduced her friend, Johnny Dupris, a classmate she'd been dating for the past few years.

"Johnny, these are my American friends, Freddy and Manny. They're software app developers. Am I right?"

They both nodded.

"Yo, man. What's up?" Freddy feigned a smile and extended his hand.

"Same here, dude," Manny obliged.

After a few intros, the conversation turned to the latest in nanotech production and the coming "Great Singularity," a silly theory they subscribed to when machine and humanity would merge, dissolving all flaws and data-driven malware, destroying all inhibitions that kept people from enjoying the pleasures of collective life—love, happiness, and the bullshit pursuit of knowledge for knowledge's sake. After the small talk, Hadley looked rather bored and fidgety, playing with her keys.

"Do you guys need a ride back to your apartment?" Hadley asked.

"There's no need," Freddy replied.

"Don't worry, love," Johnny said. "I'll walk them to the car so they can get their stuff. It'll only take a second." Hadley smiled, tossed Johnny the keys, and bid the boys farewell with a hearty hug. Johnny asked if he could see their expensive skateboards. They traded admirable tidbits and banter about the French scene and how long they intended to stay. It was weird for Manny and Freddy, who felt embarrassed and ashamed. How could they have fallen so deep as to think their friendship had cracks? Johnny asked whether getting high on the rush of skateboarding was addictive. Freddy nudged Manny at the awkwardness of Johnny's questions and wondered what was happening. Was Johnny on the level about skateboarding? More questions.

And then Johnny popped a question: Did they want some magic dust?

Freddy smirked and said, "I'm game, but I ain't got the coin."

"Same here," Manny added.

Not deterred, Johnny got out some packets, cut open a few, and gave them a few whiffs, and they snorted. A few minutes later, they got near Hadley's parked car. And Johnny noticed the skateboards.

Almost as an afterthought, Johnny took Manny's skateboard, plopped it on the pavement, and started playing with it. He made a few flips.

"Hey, man. It ain't a toy," Freddy quipped.

Johnny wasn't listening because he was jamming to the music coming from his earbuds. It was all dreamlike. They could see Johnny slide fast on the skateboard, like some mannequin dangling with invisible strings from the sky, all in Manny's mind. Freddy giggled as he saw Johnny swerving past traffic, his head bobbing, oblivious to honking horns and buzzing traffic.

Hadley was too far away, paying the café waiter as the Parisian night traffic grew thicker. More people crowded the sidewalk, and tourist buses started blocking intersections. But Johnny ignored them, weaving in and out, doing flips and somersaults, spinning like a top, while jamming to loud noise from his earbuds. Freddy and Manny watched an enormous tour bus lurch toward them as Johnny glided past, showing off his skateboarding skills.

"Hey, hey! Look out," Manny said as the large tour bus barreled down the boulevard. Freddy grabbed Manny's arm, preventing him from reaching out to Johnny as the panicked bus driver honked his horn. Like some slow-motion flick, the bus slammed against Johnny as Manny and Freddy watched the skateboard flip up into the air, almost surreal in slow motion, and poor Johnny, like a broken marionette, slammed against a barrier, smashing his skull against the curb.

A crowd gathered. Hadley saw people rushing to the intersection near her parked car. They all ran to the accident scene, but Johnny was long gone. Freddy and Manny were speechless after seeing Hadley huddled beside Johnny Dupris's frail body. Sirens screamed from afar. Soon, the gendarmes would come and ask questions.

But that's not what went down.

Johnny was far from the accident, and the magic dust had created a wishful vision in both Manny and Freddy. They resented Johnny as the interloper who made them look foolish and silly, thinking Hadley would even consider them boyfriend material. It was all in their head, and demeaning to believe that they would betray their friendship for Hadley. Johnny gave them their shakeboards and wished them well. They still looked dazed and confused.

Johnny walked up to Hadley and placed his arms around her. The boys waved a final goodbye to Hadley and Johnny.

"I think we need to split, Manny."

"Yeah, I guess you're right."

They glided down the sidewalks on their skateboards, passing tourists, the lights glistening as Paris had often changed the lives of so many.

PSYCHOANALYSIS

I entered her office and saw the room brightly lit, with floor-to-ceiling bookcases and a mahogany desk with an emerald-green desk lamp, reminiscent of those found in the Boston Public Library. She smiled and began our session. It was my second meeting, and she asked me to bring something from my past to discuss.

Dr. Stacia Evans was her name, and she came highly recommended. I was scanning the books and saw hefty tomes of Freud, Jung, Horney, and other unfamiliar names. We spoke briefly about our sessions and then began my consultation.

"Let's get started," she said. "Do you have something to show me or talk about?"

"Yes, of course," I said, and opened my briefcase and removed my high school yearbook, which also contained a copy of one of my favorite novels.

When I recall my school days, I remember being struck by a cryptic line from William Faulkner's novel A *Light in August*. Reading brought me great joy back then as I tried to become a writer in a world where I seldom found stories written by people like me. I copied down sentences from D.H. Lawrence, enticing, even if they were a bit over the top in terms of salaciousness and outward eroticism. Still, Faulkner's sentences aligned with Victorian prudery and were elusive regarding sensuality.

Memory believes before knowing remembers.

The Faulknerian sentence was intriguing because of its boldness: Memory believes before knowing remembers. That strange, befuddling sentence lit up like a burning bush. I read it repeatedly, trying to decipher its cryptic message, "Memory believes?" Is he referring to preconsciousness in a Freudian sense? Or was he just being erudite, trying to instill a passion for the Greek ideal? Still, I shelved it in my memory glands for later use, as it might be resurrected many years later.

Dr. Evans scribbled something into her journal. She asked me to open the yearbook.

That sense of awe returned when I flipped through a yearbook. It was before my high school reunion, and a friend had loaned me the yearbook because I hadn't purchased it due to a lack of funds. Scanning through it, a picture of a girl caught my attention. I struggled to read her name, as the tiny lettering beneath the picture was smudgy at best. Then I remembered her—Urelia Mendoza.

"And why do you remember her?" Dr. Evans asked.

I extended the yearbook to her, and she cradled it in her arms. She looked closely and grabbed her glasses. She stared at the picture intently, then turned to me, and I said, "Sadly, I can't say I do. She is not strikingly beautiful, but they all look somewhat familiar."

She asked me if I had ever been hypnotized, and I said no. She said it would help me remember why I found that woman so attractive. She took out a gold key light and asked me to lie back on the couch and concentrate on the light. The room darkened, and I could see the light glowing and ebbing, and her voice soothing and relaxing. I stared at the light, counting to fifty as she guided me with her gentle voice. My eyelids grew heavy.

She told me to take a mental picture of the yearbook, and then, in my mind, I turned page after page until I saw a picture of Mr. Wilson. A grizzled old man with ruddy cheeks and a bulbous nose. Old Man Wilson taught ninth-grade math. He had a nasty habit of clearing his throat in between blackboard equations. He'd get all worked up, talking about integers and slopes, his raspy voice suppressing a gooey buildup of phlegm in his esophagus, ready to deliver a wallop. For these occasions, he kept an empty red coffee can on the floor of the blackboard.

As kids, we knew what was coming whenever we heard that wet, guttural sound. The guys giggled, and the girls squirmed in their seats when they saw the stringy moco dangling from his bulbous nose. Previous classmates had warned us about his nasty habit. They said that if he misses the can, beware; ground zero will become a gooey mess. The girls winced and clenched their teeth, while the boys sitting in the back cheered and hollered, "Touchdown!" It was quite a sight.

One kid even shouted: "*Pinche Mocos*! I scored ten points!"

"Settle down, boys; I know what you're saying," he'd say.

Old Man Wilson also sponsored *The Hawkeye*, a student newspaper.

As the student editor, I'd arrive at school early and enter the office on the first Friday of each month. In a far corner sat the big, gray mimeograph machine, which printed our newsletter. Next to that office was the cafeteria.

Back then, we spoke a mishmash of Spanish and English. Many kids dropped out and never made it to high school. The use of English was strictly enforced. Hall monitors patrolled the school grounds to implement English language supremacy. Anyone caught speaking Spanish was charged a penny a word for language violations. Assimilation was the name of the game. The school had a few good teachers and an abundance of bad ones. Of course, Wilson was one of the better ones. His grandfatherly appearance displayed a warm glow of *cariño*, a cultural kindness reserved for those who respected Latino culture.

I remember sitting one morning in the cafeteria with my best friend, Julian. We were munching on our tacos when this girl sauntered to our table. Uriela Mendoza was her name. She was an attractive girl with wide eyes, an enchanting smile, and a body shaped like a Coke bottle. I figured she was aiming at Julian, but he was taken aback when she leaned over, cupped her hand to my ear, and whispered, "You have a tear on your zipper."

My brows furrowed, thinking, A what? A tear—like torn pants? My mind scrambled desperately, with utter confusion about what to do. I sat there paralyzed. She said the girls across our table could see a sliver of whiteness on my crotch, even though I was wearing black pants. I looked away and slowly, without her noticing, slid my hand to confirm her claim. Don't blush, she said. She was right. I felt the tear and the softness of my cotton briefs. She said she could patch it lickety-split. I sat quietly, and then she touched my shoulder, opened her purse, and showed me her sewing kit.

"See, I'm gonna take care of it."

I nodded.

Julian was quietly ignoring us. When Uriela strolled back to the girls, Julian quickly nudged me, whispering, "What did Uranus want?"

He loved tagging girls with weird names.

"She wants to fix my pants. She says I've got a tear near my zipper," I said.

"A what? A hole in your pants?"

He scowled.

"She even pointed out the whiteness of my briefs," I added.

He looked dumbfounded, shaking his head. And then he asked, "You didn't tell her, yes?"

"I did."

"That was stupid. What if it's a trap?"

"A trap—huh?"

"Maybe they want to steal your pants and leave you naked. Who knows?"

I didn't respond and wondered why she would do that. She said it was all straightforward in a mundane way: All I had to do was remove my pants in the boy's bathroom, give them to her, and she'd sew them in no time. It was a harmless idea. Deep down, though, it *was* a stupid idea when you think about it.

"Why don't you just go home?" Julian said.

It was getting late, and the first-period bell was about to ring.

Against his advice, I allowed Urelia to mend the pants. I rushed upstairs to the boys' restroom with Julian as my wingman and Uriela trailing behind. I removed my pants and gave them to Julian, who, in turn, gave them to Urelia. He waited outside and made sure I wouldn't be interrupted.

Once inside, I snuck into a stall and waited and waited until I heard footsteps shuffling into the restroom. Whoever it was made an ugly, nasal sound, cleared his throat, and spat into a basin. Oh my gosh, not him. I was sitting on a toilet seat when the stall door opened.

"Can I have some privacy, please?"

Old Man Wilson was startled, raised his bushy eyebrows, and said, "I'm not going to ask what you are doing because I know I won't believe it. Just don't be late to class—and wear some pants, for Pete's sake."

He slammed the door and left.

Some guys went in and wondered what the hell was going on, but Julian kept them at bay and hustled them out. Five minutes took a long time. Finally, there was a knock on the door, and Julian returned my pants, saying, "You're lucky—just in time."

The misadventure was all but forgotten.

Memories like that are unforgettable and become entwined as the years pass. I read somewhere that Sigmund Freud believed trauma can distort memory and disguise it as some psychological complex. Years later, that face and that memory came tumbling into the present. I was teaching an undergraduate class at Our Lady of the Lake College and had just finished covering *Oedipus the King*, emphasizing Aristotle's concept of Catharsis. I walked to the elevator. Students were milling around the elevator as classes had ended. My peripheral vision caught an attractive woman staring at me. I glanced, trying to recognize her, but couldn't place her face. She had porcelain skin, dark eyes, and crimson lipstick. She sauntered, smiled, and said, "Well, hello, stranger! It's been a long, long time. Remember me?"

She had perfect white teeth. My mind was racing to connect a name to the face.

I struggled, thinking, until a bell rang in my head.

"Ahh, Cooper Junior High," I said.

"Bingo! You remembered. I see you've become a teacher?"

"Yeah, I teach humanities."

"Well, do you remember me?"

"It's Uriela Mendoza, correct?"

"Gonzalez got married."

The elevator doors opened; we entered. She spoke about our junior high days, mentioned some forgotten classmates, and then asked if I wanted to share a Coke. The autumn air was nippy. I told her I had to get home early because I didn't want my wife to worry, and she said the same thing about her husband. She talked her head off about her life and then asked me, unexpectedly, if I remembered the incident about the pants. She said it so off the cuff.

"Oh, that," I smiled. "All junior high drama."

She laughed.

"I remember when you fixed the torn pants," I added.

She cracked a broad smile and told me the torn zipper exposed the white underwear like a tongue beckoning them to act on it. She even pointed out that I was sitting with Julian in the cafeteria. She said the girls all giggled until one of them said I had to be told before class started.

"I volunteered to tell Julian," Urelia said.

The pupils of her eyes widen, flashing her teeth like a Cheshire Cat. And then, almost like an afterthought, she blurted that she would have loved to go out with me to see what it was like and wondered if I had any regrets. All this was happening too fast. She was getting edgy, and I was nervous. I glanced at my watch and said, "I think it's getting late. I'd better head home."

Right there, I caught the mistake. "Wait a minute, what do you mean, tell Julian?"

She smiled, "Of course, silly. Julian had the torn pants, and you convinced him to remove them while we sewed them. It was all rather innocent."

"But? All this time, I thought."

"Let's drive to the park to share more stories."

She looked amazing in her tight red dress, and I could see her cleavage. It was getting dark. Against my better judgment, I uttered: "Well, ah, a few minutes wouldn't hurt."

I followed her to the parking garage, where she got into a black Mercedes SUV. She drove to a secluded area while I followed closely, parking beside her driver's window. She lowered her window and said, "Come on over, I won't bite." I bit my underlip and plunged ahead; opening the passenger door, I sat down. She pressed a button, and the seats reclined. The dark-tinted windows made the outside darker.

"We never finished our business," she said.

"Business?"

"You never thanked me for patching his pants. Do you also

wear white underwear?" She stared right at me with a frisky grin. I took a long gulp, pretending everything was fine. She inched over to me to get something from the glove compartment at that moment. Leaning forward, she grabbed my crotch and pulled me toward her. My heart was beating fast. She closed her eyes and opened her mouth. She wasn't wasting time. I felt her soft hands around me. "I knew you were good the minute I saw you," she said.

I closed my eyes and felt the wetness of her mouth. Crazy thoughts were going through my mind. I was afraid of park rangers. I felt tingling when she tightened her grip; moments later, I could hear her pleasing moans. She finished, grabbed a napkin from the glove compartment, and wiped her mouth.

"That was delicious," she said.

I smiled, thinking how unbelievable this was.

"I don't know what to say."

"Next time we can go to my house."

"Your house? But your husband? The kids!"

"He'll be gone for two weeks for reserve training, and the kids are away at college."

Recovered memories are part fantasy, mostly libido-driven. Perhaps Freud is correct in saying that some parts of memory are wish-fulfillment, while the knowing is bland and ordinary. The remembering part is clouded with imagined events, and I wanted to remember it that way, but that's not how it went.

We met by accident near the college elevator. I was leaving my evening class when she saw me and uttered my name. I turned around and stared at her momentarily, struggling to focus on her. And then, eureka! I said her name, and we talked briefly. She smiled and invited me to Jim's Coffee Shop, a few blocks off campus. I looked at my watch and said, 'Okay.' Minutes later, she parked her black SUV not far from my Volvo. I followed her, and then we took a cozy booth and ordered coffee. We chatted about junior high, and she told me she was majoring in business and wanted to start a sportswear line. I can't recall what she did for a living.

More things became apparent. Urelia was a high achiever at school—a straight shooter. She was a Catholic girl with virginity stamped on her forehead and a body waiting to be consummated by wedding vows. At Cooper, she was the do-gooder who followed all the rules and went to church on Sundays.

"I wanted to thank you for sewing Julian's pants," I said.

She furrowed her eyebrows, giving me a puzzled look, saying, "What on earth are you talking about?" Embarrassed, I stuttered and added, "Eighth grade, remember? The big hole in his crotch. You sewed his black pants. You approached me and said the girls could see his briefs like a white tongue."

"Oh my gosh, you do have an imagination."

She recomposed herself, laughed loudly, and remembered, saying, "I had all but forgotten that crazy incident." After I filled in more details, Uriela recalled the event differently. She told Elena that she had spotted the white bulge and convinced her to approach me about sewing the pants. The girls argued against it because it was a big no-no. The girls of that time held conserva-tive ideas about propriety and decorum. But Elena insisted.

"You know, Elena had a serious crush on you," Urelia said.

Elena evoked strange feelings, as I had forgotten about her until Urelia brought her name into focus. Of course, I snapped, the girl with the gray eyes, long eyelashes, and beige skin. She was always being sent home because of her red stilettos. Julian had dubbed them CFM shoes. The school dress code was strictly enforced, and Elena was usually in the Vice-Principal's office for wearing inappropriate garments and shoes. She was the outrageous one. Who could forget a face that launched a thousand school fights?

"I didn't know she had a crush on me."

"Oh, yes, she did! You were the big man on campus!"

She added, "Student Council, newspaper editor, tennis team hotshot!"

I looked away.

"Don't blush," she added.

She said it was Elena who shoved a sewing kit into her purse and begged her to go over and tell me about the hole in Julian's crotch. Then Uriela agreed. She got up from her little group, meandered to my area, and whispered in my ear. All the while, Julian looked dazed and confused.

"Your friend Julian was like a pit bull. What was up with him, anyway?"

"Ohh, Jay. Overprotective, I guess. We're still buddies after all this time."

"So, why didn't you let Elena take the lead?" I asked.

She explained that Elena was the competitive one who usually got what she wanted. She said that whenever she wore a red bikini to a public pool, Elena would wear an even skimpier one. I remembered Elena because she lived just a few blocks from my house, and I vividly recall attending her birthday party one day in fifth grade. After she cut the cake, she turned around and kissed me on the cheek. All the kids laughed and cheered. I was embarrassed and swore that I would never speak to her again.

Things changed in junior high.

Urelia said she wanted to do something bold and get Elena jealous. When Julian gave the girls my pants, Elena quickly sewed them. Right here, the plot thickens because once Elena finished, Urelia snatched them from her hands and dashed to the boy's restroom to hand them to me. Julian was already in the boys' bathroom, and I was standing guard. I blocked her, saying it was off-limits. Only I could return them to Julian. Uriela smiled and said, "As you wish."

At about this time, I stared at my watch.

"I think I ought to head home. It's getting late."

"Wait a minute. I want to do something." Urelia said she'd always wanted to do something brave outside her comfort zone. All her life, missed chances and squandered opportunities became a gauzy world of should-haves.

"All these years, I thought about you and wondered how long it had been," Urelia said.

"Just seeing you brought back a flood of memories."

Uriela was insistent that I repay her kindness. She added that Julian had the hots for Elena from the get-go, even though the girl rejected him. She inferred that Julian had made moves toward her, too. I doubted all this because Julian never mentioned Elena or Urelia, as he was starstruck by this girl from another school. The girl was far classier and prettier than any of the girls from Cooper.

"I think you got it all wrong. I've known Julian for decades. He never told me about this?"

She was fidgeting with her wedding band, her pupils widening. She smiled and said we should pack up and head home. The red lip imprint on the coffee rim and her perfect white teeth made me wonder what else was in store for me.

"I think it's getting late," I said.

"Walk me to my car. I want to show you something in private."

I paid the bill, and we left the restaurant into the chilly night air.

She had parked her dark SUV in a corner. Crazy thoughts were going through my mind. I imagined Uriela opening the vehicle door, suddenly turning and kissing me. I could almost feel her warm body and the smooth touch of her hands on my face.

"Get inside for just a few minutes."

It wasn't a suggestion but a command; she was used to giving orders.

I thought about the many missed opportunities and wondered what was in store for me. "Close your eyes," she said.

"But, but..."

"Shhhh."

With my eyes shut, she touched my shoulder and sighed deeply. I imagined her saying, 'I remember holding your pants, taking a long whiff, and smelling the ocean.' The whiteness of the tongue dared me. I wanted it so bad." An image of the roaring ocean slamming the shoreline, the foamy crashing waves, and Aphrodite atop a seashell came into focus.

"Open your eyes," she said.

She was smiling and holding the sewing kit she had taken from her glove compartment.

Ohh, I muttered.

It was the same sewing kit from years ago.

"I'm prepared," she laughed. "I dreamt that one day we'd meet and talk about those crazy days at Cooper Junior High."

"Remember Mr. Wilson?" I asked.

Her eyes welled up with tears. She shared the saddest thing about Old Man Wilson—he had died of esophageal cancer, but kept a strict diet despite his weakness. He loved teaching. Uriela, who was in his advisory, said that the Old Man felt so compassionate about teaching and believed everyone was entitled to the American Dream. The idea of the coffee can came from his students, who weren't embarrassed by his illness. The guys oppressed Mr. Wilson by their mean tricks. A wave of sadness and guilt suddenly overtook me, and for some strange reason, my thoughts drifted to Old Man Wilson and his bulbous nose with snot dripping into the red coffee can.

And right at the moment, I mentioned the red can, I opened my eyes. Everything came into focus.

I saw the room brightly lit, with floor-to-ceiling bookcases and a mahogany desk with an emerald-green desk lamp, reminiscent of those found in the Boston Public Library. Dr. Amelia

Evans repeated the phrase, *Memory believes before knowing remembers.*

It seemed a full hour had passed, and Dr. Evans said, "Your story is provocative, as it does give you clues as to why you remembered it?"

"I see what you mean?"

"The bulbous nose, red can, red dress, and the name of Urelia Mendoza. These are all symbolic items, cryptically phallic," she added.

"But why do I have two accounts of the same story?"

"You tell me?" I thought about stitching the stories together, and then it occurred to me.

"My first wife was a seamstress, but deep down, we weren't right for each other, so we divorced. Her mother's name was Aurelia, and maybe her name is mixed up with strange thoughts."

"What strange thoughts," Dr. Evans asked.

"She wore red lipstick and used to be a dancer."

I froze and looked away, staring at a statue of Artemis holding the sacred deer on the desk next to the green lamp.

"At our next session, I want you to consider why you gave Aurelia the strange surname of Mendacity." *Memory believes before knowing remembers.*

MARFA LIGHTS

"**Y**ou're going too fast!"

"I'm driving the speed limit."

"You ain't. It's supposed to be 65 miles an hour," she said.

"It's 90 miles!"

"That's the highway sign, you numbskull!"

"Oh."

A long pause before he released his heavy foot from the gas pedal. The speedometer needle slumped down to 75. He believed the cops never stopped anyone going just 10 miles over the speed limit. He'd been pressing the pedal to the metal because he needed to find a McDonald's to go piss.

Joseph Adam McCabe and his wife, Wilma, had been married for thirty-five years. They were on their way to see the Marfa lights. And, of course, to celebrate and honor the legendary story of a UFO that descended on the town in 1883 when Grandpa Amos McCabe and Grandma Fredericka had been traveling south on a buckboard to visit relations who lived on the outskirts. The old couple panicked when a bright, luminous light flooded their wagon, and Sara, their mule, bucked and unhitched herself, leaving them stranded.

The McCabes interpreted this incident as a sign from Ezekiel, with the Wheel of Light shooting off fireworks the likes of which no mortal had seen in their lifetime.

The story had been passed down through the McCabes' family, and Joseph was going to the courthouse with a letter from the Texas Land Commissioner asking the city fathers to erect a historical marker.

But that never happened. Joseph and Wilma never got there because he fell asleep at the wheel. They awoke strapped to gurneys with tubes running down their noses. The hospital staff said some folks had found them unconscious, engulfed in a blue, luminous light, making a humming noise.

Like most stories, this one is based on hearsay and twice-told tales that have become convoluted and twisted. Even the story of Grandpa Amos wasn't exactly true because Old Amos loved to take a few swigs from a corn-whisky jug, and Fredericka usually dozed off during those long journeys and couldn't remember what day of the week, if her life depended on it.

The way it happened was that Amos and Fredericka were Holy Rollers, who believed the Apocalypse was nearing because their pastor, Rev. Goodwin, said all signs pointed to the coming of the Great Rapture. They had gotten lost, and poor Sara had gotten unhitched and wandered off. The tale had entered the annals of urban legends and Area 51 stories.

But when the McCabes drove their station wagon into that dusty, circular gravel driveway that led to the Old Amos and Fredericka homestead, the place was empty. The doors unlocked. The windows were wide open with curtains billowing as if inviting strangers to sit a spell. Wilma wandered to the kitchen while Joseph went upstairs.

"Papa!" Wilma shouted. "You're not gonna believe this."

"What in tarnation!"

"They left us cornbread and taters with chicken on the pot boiler."

Joseph came trotting down the stairs. He was hungry for home cooking. After that long meal, Joe set about to investigate, while Wilma washed dishes and looked around. The barn was empty, and there was no sign of life. They knew it was the right place because of old photographs hanging in the living room of long-lost relatives and a faded sepia photo of Grandpa Amos McCabe, with his long, fluffy beard and wide-brimmed hat, looking like Walt Whitman in the old pictures of the famous Bard. By nightfall, the cool breeze chilled the homestead. Amos had passed his property to Moses, his youngest.

Common in small towns, Sheriff Arty Stone kept a steady vigil on vacant homesteads in his jurisdiction. From the highway, he spotted a yellowish glow coming from inside the house and was duty-bound to investigate. As his patrol vehicle drew closer, he saw an elderly couple cleaning up the area. He knew the bank had begun foreclosure proceedings.

"Howdy folks, what seems to be the problem?"

"Evening, Sheriff," Joseph said. Wilma continued her business, trying to improve the place.

"Are you related to the McCabes?"

"That's old grandpappy. I'm Joseph McCabe, and this here is Wilma. Mamma!" Wilma turned around, smiled, and went back to cleaning up the place. Sheriff Stone was busy eyeing the photos on the wall.

The stranger's voice did remind Arty of Old Moses. He even looked like the pictures hanging on the living room. He knew this because Stone had spent many Saturdays drinking coffee with Old Moses McCabe and his wife, Eunice. They were direct descendants of Amos and Fredericka. As was Joseph McCabe, Moses' favorite nephew.

It had been a month now since the McCabe place had been vacant, and the town fathers wanted to straighten out the homestead before placing it on the market. Sheriff Stone ensured that no squatters laid claim to it under the old Homestead Act. The bank had already chased off some individuals who were attempting to place liens on the property.

"Are you laying claim to the place? You do know that they packed up and left with no word to the bank," Sheriff Stone said.

"Yup."

"And the strangest thing," Stone added, "even the farm animals are gone. No tire tracks. No visible signs of forced entry. Nothing. Like they—"

"Vanished into thin air, Sheriff?" Joseph interrupted.

"You could say that. I mean, we investigated the matter thoroughly."

"Just like Ezekiel had prophesied. They got whisked up into a fiery wheel. That's the story of them?"

"I ain't going that far. I put no faith in myths."

He didn't tell the Sheriff that the place had been occupied and the people had left in a hurry.

"I'll tell you, Sheriff. Come Monday morning, I'm heading to town to meet with the bank and settle all past accounts."

"That's mighty fine. In the meantime, I'll be passing by to see if you need anything."

"Stop by anytime for coffee," Joseph added. The idea made the Sheriff smile at the hospitality, and he thought about Old Moses before leaving quickly because his radio had transmitted a 451. The sheriff sped away with his flashing emergency lights on.

Joseph and Wilma took stuff out of their station wagon, and the place was becoming livable again. When night settled, the old place made strange whirling noises coming from the rooftop. Tumbleweeds scattered like travelling vagabonds with the faraway howl of coyotes vying for their attention.

Wilma had never been bothered by night noises, but tonight

was different. She kept tossing and turning, jittered by bad dreams while Old Joseph snored away. She got up during the night and checked all the doors. She looked out the kitchen window and saw a strange blinking green light. The pulsing green light changed to orange, then back to green, followed by yellow, and finally royal blue. She'd never seen such a thing. Wilma ran back to the bedroom and woke up Joseph.

"What now, Wilma. For God's sake."

"There's something strange out there. Someone's playing a game, sending us messages," Wilma uttered.

"Go back to sleep."

"Please, Joseph."

He tossed off the bedcovers and found his slippers, then shuffled to the bathroom. Wilma was getting impatient. He grumbled for his glasses and waddled to the kitchen with Wilma right behind him. He peeked out. And there it was: a blinking green eyeball, changing colors as if beckoning them.

"I'm going out to investigate," Joseph said.

"You'll do no such thing. Call the Sheriff."

"Ain't gonna bother him. He'll think we're nuts."

It was settled. Old Joseph grabbed a flashlight and ventured into the darkness to discover what the blinking green light was. Old Wilma walked right behind him with a two-by-four ready for any surprises. The stars made the night sky beautiful, and the surrounding area was vacant, except for adobe houses separated by a vast expanse of arid emptiness. A strange coldness embraced them as they got closer to the blinking light. They were near a dry arroyo and close to a hillside. Just darkness. His flashlight shot a straight beam of light.

"It's getting colder, Joe," Wilma said, clinging closer to Joseph.

"It's just you, Mama. You've just got those hot flashes."

She gave him a little shove, and then froze when she touched a tumbleweed. She felt the frost on its prickly surface. "Well, what's this?" Wilma grazed Joseph's face with the thin ice on her hand.

Before he could say anything, the humming noise grew louder, and the strange, glowing light just hovering above the ground changed colors again. This time, it was a reddish-orange, pulsing like a throbbing heartbeat. It was moving toward them. Or were they moving towards it?

They couldn't tell.

"Great Caesar's ghost, what the hell?" Joseph uttered. Wilma clung closer to him.

"Oh, Holy Jesus, what is it?"

The green light surrounded them. They felt the throbbing against their skin, like cool water flowing around them, yet dry and serene. He'd imagine it like those Jacuzzis rich people have in their homes. Wilma felt tingly and had goosebumps around her arms and legs; Joseph felt a strange longing for Wilma right before they eloped. It was both satisfying and forbidding. They embraced tightly. The green light did a miraculous thing. Joseph and Wilma had become younger than they had been before; their skin had transformed into that of young teenagers, and they laughed and giggled, unable to believe their eyes. They never felt so happy, like kids with new toys. Their old clothes felt loose and smelly.

They looked back at the house, and it was no longer there. The surroundings felt eerily familiar. A green glow surrounded them, causing their skin to appear green and then blue. Joseph looked at Wilma and saw a young girl with twinkling eyes, beautiful lips, and a scent of apple blossom. She looked at Joseph and saw his teeth white, his ears smaller, and the double chin gone. An irresistible scent of lavender and musk lingered on his body, constantly driving her crazy for him. He was a bit taller now, his breeches looser, and his eyes brighter.

"Joe make love to me," Wilma said.

He smiled and laid an intense kiss. They fell on the green

ground, happy and elated with wild abandonment. The whole area was glowing green, sparkly and pulsing, the humming noise evoking a sense of wanderlust inside the belly of Mother Earth. They made love. They fell asleep.

That morning, they found themselves back in a place from their childhood—no green light. The vacant plain felt strangely different. Wilma remembered it as strange, as though time had stopped, and Joseph thought about his mother and how she might be upset that he hadn't finished his chores around the barn. They looked and laughed. "This is crazy," Wilma said.

"What?" Joseph asked.

I just heard King barking.

"That's impossible. He's been dead for decades."

Before she could say another word, a German shepherd came frolicking and wagging its tail, happy to see Wilma and Joe. Their old house was over the hilltop.

"King, my sweetie!" Wilma cried. She had grieved him so much when her father had put him down. Joe petted him and rubbed his belly. Before long, Joseph heard Mildred Staggs, his mother-in-law, who had died of cancer. Wilma couldn't believe what she was hearing coming from beyond the hill.

It just couldn't be.

They looked at themselves, and they were wearing different clothing, and both looked innocent. The woman suddenly appeared above the hill with an apron. Her arms crossed.

"There I found you two. Come on, it's getting late."

Mildred knew all along where the lovebirds had wandered off. Then she pointed at Joseph, saying, "Joe, your dad needs you to finish your chores."

"Yes, ma'am," Joseph said, embarrassed.

Wilma smiled at Joseph and walked away with her mother, with King tagging along. Joseph knew where to go because he lived with his grandpa Moses, who had raised him as a young boy after his father died in the war. But he remembered

Mildred saying that his dad was looking for him. That was impossible. His dad never returned from the war, and he had been barely thirteen years old when his father's body was shipped back from France. He sauntered, glancing around at his surroundings, and saw Mildred and Wilma shrinking into a speck as they moved closer to their home. He noticed Wilma turning around and waving at him, with King running in circles around them.

It took a while before Joseph got closer to the homestead. He opened the kitchen door and saw Grandpa Moses smiling, and he hugged him.

"I thought you were lost, Joey," Grandpa Moses said.

"Your Dad wants to say goodbye. He's shipping out tomorrow," he added.

"Okay, Gramps," the words came out naturally.

From the corner of the bedroom, his father emerged. He wore his olive-drab Army uniform and stood tall, with a chiseled square jaw and deep-set brown eyes. The golden oak leaves on his shoulders glistened, giving his father an authoritative presence. His mother had long passed away in a car accident. As a career military officer, the boy had stayed with his grandparents.

"Joseph, I want you to do everything Grampa and Grandma say, you hear." He gave his son a strong hug and then left.

"I'll be back in no time."

Those were the last words from his father before he left, and his parents took him to the Marfa Auxiliary Army Airfield. Joseph stayed behind to care for the house and repair the windmill. He went off to see Wilma, and there, he felt that strange, eerie sensation. The sky had turned a bluish dark, with a cool breeze picking up alongside strange, rumbling clouds. A flash of lightning zigzagged across the sky, followed by a clap of thunder. He feared dark funnels swooping down like dust devils.

The glowing green light beckoned him. He wondered if

Wilma had spotted the dust devils, too, since it was closer to her area above the hilltop. He walked faster until something told him to hurry up, and Joseph increased his steady pace. From afar, he saw Wilma running from her house with her arms extended. Lightning cracked the sky, followed by a heavy boom. Wilma was now closer to the green light as Joseph finally caught up, and they both embraced.

"I've missed you, Joe," Wilma said. She kissed him, and Joseph said, "We need to go back."

"No, I can't. I won't go back." She was frantic.

"It's our only chance. We don't belong here."

"We can stay here and start all over. We know the future," Wilma said.

"It wasn't meant to be."

"Why are we here, then? God's given us another chance, darling. Don't you see!" Wilma was stubborn. She felt the pull of her parents, and seeing her King again was a double joy.

The humming sound grew stronger. The water streaming down their bodies intensified. Their skin loosened, like fat melting away, and Joseph could see his hands becoming bony, bluish veins standing out against his skin, along with worry lines and wrinkles appearing. Wilma broke away from his grasp and screamed, "Joey, Joseph. Come back!" Within seconds, Wilma was gone. The humming stopped. The greenish light faded into a weak bluish glow, and then it disappeared.

Joseph lay on the ground, his thoughts racing back to Wilma. He wondered if it was all just a bad dream. He trudged back to the house, envisioning everything returning to normal, with Wilma opening the door. But then he recalled the strange Marfa lights. When he opened the door, all was quiet. Nothing stirred. Not even the sound of silence. Wilma was gone.

A few minutes later, Sheriff Stone knocked on the door. He peeked through the curtains and saw him.

"Sheriff Stone? Back so soon."

"Sorry to bother you. We got a report of strange lights coming from your area."

"Lights? What lights?"

"Is your friend at home?"

"What friend?"

"That girl I saw you with going up the hill?" Sheriff Stone said.

What the Sheriff didn't tell him was that he'd seen Joseph and this young girl from his cruiser using his night-vision binoculars. He wondered what they were up to. It all seemed very suspicious.

Joseph gathered some coffee grounds and brewed a fresh pot of coffee. He was pouring water into the percolator when Sheriff Stone commented, "Kinda strange, you ask me."

"Look, Sheriff, if I told you. You wouldn't believe me."

"Try me," Sheriff Stone said. He plunked down on a green sofa.

"You see, Wilma, my wife. You remember her when I introduced her to you. Remember?" Joseph said. "She went with me, and that strange light just snatched her out of my arms."

Sheriff Stone scratched his head and gave him a strange look. "I don't remember you introducing me to any Wilma. You were here alone, and I asked you what your intentions were regarding the McCabe property. That's all."

"But she was tidying up the place," Joseph said.

"Nope. Why don't you go with me to my office so we can record this?" Sheriff Stone shrugged.

"Now listen here, Sheriff. I don't know what all this is about. But I lost my Wilma out there." Joseph was getting agitated. Sheriff Stone radioed in for 906 (officer needs assistance).

"Why don't we talk about this at the station, Mr. McCabe. We'll organize a search party and find that missing person. How about that?"

"Don't you patronize me, goddammit! I won't have that!"

Joseph was losing it. He looked around for any clothing or items that would justify her identity. He even thought about looking for her purse. But there was no trace of any of her belongings. Then he remembered that if Wilma had selected to stay, then, logically, she'd been erased from his time. Everything had changed. Sheriff Stone wouldn't have remembered her.

"Sheriff, I can explain everything."

"Good, let's do so. Please turn around."

"Do you have to do that?"

"Just standard protocol."

He handcuffed him and placed McCabe in the backseat while a Texas DPS cruiser finally drove up beside his vehicle.

"Everything okay, Stone?" the trooper asked.

"Everything under control. Thank you."

The ride to the station was a long one. Sheriff Stone drove for a good forty minutes.

Not a single word was exchanged. As McCabe entered the station, he glanced over at their logo: City of Marfa Police: Home of the Mystery Lights."

Sheriff Stone uncuffed him. To his surprise, one of the female attendants was a gal by the name of Wilma Murphy.

"Do I know you? You sure look familiar?"

"This here is Joseph McCabe, relative of Moses McCabe at the old homestead," Sheriff Stone said.

Joseph was speechless, shouting: "Wilma! It's me, Joseph — you're husband!" He stared at her intensely. Wilma looked puzzled. And then it hit her like a lightning bolt.

"You're Joey McCabe! I remember now. Your grandparents lived close to our place." Wilma had always been short on words, but she flashed her wedding band; Joseph could see her name tag, "Wilma S. Murphy."

Staggs was her maiden name.

"Small town, eh," Sheriff Stone quipped.

Two more officers came up while Sheriff Stone explained a

possible homicide and wanted a search party near Stagg's property area.

"It's those Marfa lights, isn't?" Wilma said.

Joseph McCabe looked down, pinching himself, and turned to Wilma and asked, "You believe in second chances?"

BIG LUCAS A.K.A. TONINA

*T*his is a true story.

I've carried it like a seething scar across my forehead. I've read that Comanches often scarred their relatives who showed cowardice in battle. Sometimes, I feel responsible because I could have stopped it, but I didn't.

His name was Lucas Cruz. But everybody called him Tonina Jackson. The real Tonina Jackson was a rotund wrestler who made his debut in All-Star Wrestling in the early '60s. The show was telecast live from the Josephine Theatre. And just like Tonina Jackson, Lucas was big—an obese-looking guy, barely five-five.

Lucas blended in with the group like the others who attended Cooper Junior High in the 1970s. Cooper was a West-Side pipeline school to either Fox Tech or Sidney Lanier, two segregated, vocational-technical high schools that limited us to blue-collar jobs. It wasn't that bad because I had no idea what I wanted to be after high school.

At school, Big Lucas Tonina hung around the heavies—the guys who controlled the playground—the pachucos who fought each other for territorial rights to assert their dominance over the less powerful. Back then, "pachucos" were like the Jets in "West Side Story." Cliquish guys who believed toughness was a ticket to success.

The Lucas tragedy occurred during the winter of '75, when rainy days and freezing temperatures prevented us from engaging in outdoor activities. Physical Education (P.E.) was required for all junior high students. We played basketball and competed in track relays; the girls played volleyball or softball. They used to say it was just a way to let off steam.

It was Wednesday, and the rain kept us stuck indoors. Coach Covington directed us to the retractable bleachers upon our arrival at gym class. We noticed the girls had set up a corner with a portable phonograph, while Mr. Huerta, the Vice Principal, prepared a microphone and prominent speakers. The wooden floors were shiny and spotless.

"Gentlemen," Coach Covington said. "Today, we have a special treat. You're going to dance with the ladies. And you will participate." The last phrase was said with irony. He knew we didn't want to participate because we'd have to take off our shoes so that we wouldn't scuff the floors. Many of us wore torn socks or shoes with holey soles.

I dreaded it because I didn't know how to dance. The last time I tried to dance with a girl named Marta, she got all over my case for stepping on her shoes ("Just follow," she exclaimed. "I'll lead."). I looked around and headed up the creaky bleachers where Martin Gonzalez, Felipe Munoz, Cowboy Flores (the guy who always wore a cowboy hat), and Manfred (nicknamed after the cartoon character Tom Terrific) were, our goon squad.

The last to join us was Big Lucas, who came huffing and puffing because his heaviness was a burden. Martin and Felipe huddled together, whispering. I knew they were up to no good. Within earshot, I heard Manfred and Cowboy giggle. I hung out with them because they were in my homeroom advisory.

Martin turned to Tonina and said, "You know what? Janie wants you to ask her out to dance." I knew he was lying because sarcasm was etched all over his face. It was how he said it with a nasty grin curving down the corners of his mouth—like a pitbull with dark eyes.

"What?" Tonina winced. I could see Tonina was shocked. He cupped his ear, trying to hear better because the girls started playing an old hit: "Stop in the Name of Love" by the Supremes.

He shouted, "I said Janie wants you to ask her out!"

I winced. I knew it was a lie. Martin even pointed to Janie and waved to her to reassure him; she waved back from the vast distance of the gym floor.

"See, I told ya you so!" Martin said. Janie was sitting next to other girls and gossipy types. Janie probably thought Martin was drawing her attention because she had sent him a few love notes.

Janie sat in our advisory, behind Tonina, who always made small talk with her because her parents owned the grocery store where Tonina's family bought food on credit. She was a pretty brunette with hazel eyes and swung her hips dramatically. She waved at Martin again.

I knew it was all a lie and wanted to expose Martin and the others. But I just couldn't. I was hoping Lucas would come to his senses.

"You're crazy, Martin. She's just my friend," Tonina blurted out. But Martin was persistent; he couldn't let go of a good prank.

"No. No—really. She told me so," Martin insisted, ribbing Felipe, who turned to the guys and nodded in the affirmative. Cowboy and Manfred said, "Yeah, I think she does like you." They were all in on the joke.

Tonina raised his eyebrow and considered it, wondering if there was any truth to it. He had noticed lately that Janie would come out to help her parents whenever Tonina and his family came by to get groceries.

"All right, gentlemen. Let's get this show on the road!" Coach Covington said. The music was blasting loudly. Big Lucas Tonina stood up right then as the guys cheered and clapped. Covington turned around and fixed his beady eyes on Martin and Felipe, who exchanged high-fives. The boys cheered, "T-O-N-I-N-A!" Loud clapping, foot stomping, and the entire P.E. class cheered him on. After a few stern glances from Covington, the foot-stomping and cheering stopped.

Tonina waddled his way down the bleachers. You could hear his heavy breathing and the creaking of the planks as he lumbered along. The pressure from his steps sent the sitting boys flying like bowling pins. I could see his dirty socks, and the guys in the front pinched their noses.

Just then, "Just Once in My Life" by the Righteous Brothers began playing, and the girls sighed. Lucas interpreted it as a positive sign.

This was going to turn out poorly. I felt it in my bones. Lucas waddled across the shiny floor in pants so tight that lards of belly fat wiggled every step of the way. A large shadow loomed right behind him. I saw Coach Covington and Mr. Huerta huddled, whispering, and looking up at us. I could sense a bad foreboding sign and wanted to stop it. I wanted to shout, "Come back, Lucas. Don't waste your time!" Instead, I covered my face with my hands.

Across the bleachers, the girls were quiet, all bugged-eyed and staring in disbelief. The Righteous Brothers crooned to the steps of Tonia, and many of the girls were cackling like huddled hens about to lay eggs. Poor Tonina. I stared at Martin, who was unperturbed by it all with a wicked grin, relishing the intended climax.

Tonina suddenly stopped in front of a sea of faces. He looked directly at Janie, who was returning his gaze, nervously smiling.

He pointed his chubby finger at her, and she looked stunned. Time seemed to freeze. The music from the Righteous Brothers slowed to an eerie, backward moan. The girls turned toward Janie, as if saying, "Come on, get out there and support the team." Either way, her decision would change one life forever. She shook her head, probably saying, "I'm sorry, I just can't. I'm sorry, Tonina." She might have shouted it in a megaphone for everyone to hear. The gym let out a collective sigh, more like a groan. She looked more embarrassed, knowing deep down that she was wrong, but still saying no.

Tonina looked dumbfounded.

He turned red, his mouth open wide. He knew the jig was up. He had been played like a pinball. Then he made another deadly mistake by pointing to a girl next to her and another one, both of whom shook their heads, none hiding their embarrassment. The pinball backbox flashed, "Game Over!"

The guys in the bleachers laughed loudly until Coach Covington pulled out his board of education—a discipline paddle. The laughter stopped abruptly. A tense silence filled the air because everyone knew the painful consequences. Poor Tonina was slowly walking back to the bleachers, clearly upset, tears streaming down his chubby cheeks, with his head hanging in defeat.

I felt his pain of rejection.

But the show was beginning.

Coach Covington suddenly pointed to the top row and pointed out five of us: Martin, Felipe, Cowboy, Manfred, and me. I was surprised. Clearly, he was joking; I subtly pointed my finger inward, looking confused: What do you want from me?

"You, too, Gumby."

Oh my God, he gave me a nickname just because he caught me chewing bubble gum. The gum was banned because the janitors complained about cleaning the sticky residue from the wood floors, which was an unnecessary hassle.

We went down to the bottom, and the crowd was quiet. The music had stopped. Coach Vanessa, the blond-haired temptress from Odessa, was talking with the girls. She was probably scolding them.

Coach Covington pointed to the showers. We were led to where V.P. Huerta was waiting to catch the ruffians. He loved using the phrase "ruffians."

"Ok, ruffians, whose bright idea was to send Tonina out?"

Even Huerta called Lucas Tonina.

We shrugged our shoulders.

"I guess the Board of Education will loosen your tongues."

The wooden paddle was full of tiny holes. Covington liked to say it reduced the centrifugal force when swung—like we all knew what centrifugal force meant. He flexed it like a bat.

"Ruffians, lower your pants down to your knees!"

We loosened our belts and lowered our trousers. No one said anything.

"Everyone gets one lick." Coach Covington added. "Except Gumby. You get three."

This was outrageous.

"We've warned you about chewing gum," Covington said. "Over and over. G-U-M, three letters equal to three licks!"

Huerta said nothing. That was the rule.

Tonina came, and Coach Covington asked him to identify who had directed him to go out to dance. He stared at Martin and then at the others, saying nothing. He was not about to rat them out.

"Don't worry. These ruffians will get their rewards!"

I raised my hand to say a few words. I had a forged letter in my wallet reserved for these occasions; I protested the demeaning, inhumane treatment.

"Sir. I have a signed letter from my grandma saying she's against corporal punishment. You need her permission to—"

He snatched the note before I could finish my sentence.

"This is two years old. It's worthless!" He crumpled it into a ball and tossed it aside.

We bent down and touched our toes. Huerta swung the board, giving each of us one lick.

"I'll let it pass this time," Huerta whispered. "You owe me." He turned around and left in a huff.

Coach Covington scowled because Huerta amended anything he'd recommended, even rescinding the three licks rule for chewing gum.

I felt the burning sensation of a thousand wasp stings. Martin turned red, and Cowboy and Manfred were sobbing. Felipe was stoic and emotionless. I wasn't about to give pleasure to that sadistic Coach Covington. I pulled up my pants and retrieved my crumpled note. We were led out back to the gym. The dance was in full force, and we climbed onto our usual spot atop the bleachers.

Tonina stayed behind.

At homeroom advisory, I felt that burning, aching sensation. I couldn't sit still because of the aftershocks. The others endured as best they could while Cowboy and Manfred went to their advisories.

After school, I stopped for a snow cone on Tampico Street. The talk was about Tonina and the Big Rejection. That's what the gossipers called it. Rumors spread that Janie had planned the whole thing because Tonina's parents had reported the incident to the health authorities. They said the store was selling rotten meat.

But it was just that—all rumors.

That evening, the neighborhood was ablaze with flashing red lights and dozens of police officers. An ambulance with blaring sirens made its way to Tonina's home. Crowds gathered. Women in curlers and kimonos and men milling around in T-shirts, trying to discover what happened.

According to *chisme*, Tonina went home feeling ashamed of

the rejection. He tried to hang himself with an extension cord wrapped around a ceiling fan. The scene showed that the two-by-four holding the ceiling fan couldn't support his heavy weight, causing Big Tonina to fall and the ceiling fan to crash down on his head. Even the stool supporting him broke. Debris was scattered everywhere.

The story doesn't end here.

It took three men to lift the body onto a gurney. They rushed him to the county hospital in an undetermined condition. He was fighting the Grim Reaper.

Tonina didn't go back to Cooper Junior High. His parents kept him home because they worried the teasing would continue and that Lucas might try to harm himself again. His doctors put him on a protein diet, and the pounds started to melt away. Months went by. Tonina lost even more weight. He began taking Kung Fu classes at the local YMCA.

The Christmas Holidays are out until the new year. Tonina was going full steam, doing his workouts, lifting weights, crunches, and even punching a speedball.

* * *

FOUR MONTHS LATER, Lucas Cruz returned to Cooper wholly transformed. His parents had conferences with the school principal, and his homeroom advisor was changed. He looked muscular, firm, and solid. The girls said he looked like Donny Osmond. His wavy, long hair and bright eyes gave him a magazine teen-idol look, similar to those magazine headshots of angst-ridden teens. He walked confidently. The counselors refused to believe it was Tonina. Mrs. Flanders was his new advisor.

When Lucas walked in, no one recognized him as Tonina because none of the guys ever called him by his real name. His parents had asked that they refer to him as David, his middle name. Old Tonina, the big tub of guts who waddled around school, was long gone, and David Lucas Cruz had taken his place: David, the eye candy for cheerleaders and the perfect specimen for Michelangelo's nude sculptures.

A day before Spring Break, Coach Covington held a Kung Fu demonstration to gauge interest in a unique training course offered free by the neighborhood YMCA. David was the particular instructor. Only a few boys initially wanted to sign up, but they became interested when offered concert tickets and free movie passes.

Martin Gonzalez, Felipe Munoz, Cowboy, and Manfred quickly volunteered. They kept their distance from David because they couldn't remember him. When they were told, they often mistook him for Tonina's brother from Mexico. They couldn't connect the dots.

Coach Covington stood on foamy blue mats with his whistle. We all wore gym shorts and T-shirts, but David wore his black belt and white regalia. Martin was first. The gym was jam-packed. Martin was a street fighter with an ability to sucker punch if he caught you off guard. They all knew him as Dirty Martin, but no one told him that to his face.

"*Orale, ese.* Let's see what you've got," Martin cracked.

David smiled and gave him a respectful bow, clasping his hands. Covington blew his whistle.

Martin skipped and danced around David like Muhammad Ali, trying to land a punch. He moved closer to him and swung his leg toward his groin, but David was too quick. He blocked it with one hand while swinging his leg up, striking Martin in the breadbasket. Within seconds, Martin was on the floor writhing and gasping for air. He got up and tried again. After a series of kicks, Covington blew the whistle. Martin left the mat in resignation.

Next was Stoic Felipe. The same thing happened to him; he was taken out in three strikes. Cowboy and Manfred said they'd formed a tag-team match against David. Covington objected, but David agreed to the terms. Cowboy landed a few surprise punches, but not enough to win. Manfred tried his best but lost his balance when a quick kick to the jaw knocked him out. The two boys surrendered, raising their hands in submission. The fight was over. As for me, David, also known as Lucas, knew I had never been involved in that incident because I had tried to warn him.

* * *

I wish I could say this has a happy ending. But poor David Cruz was in love with the girl who had once rejected him. Fates had intervened: Janie and David became a couple. Deep down, Old Lucas had never gotten over Janie. The summer before transferring to Lanier High, Lucas confessed his identity to Janey. She already knew because his mother had told her. The two lovebirds were destined for happiness and all that jazz. But things like that only happen in fairy tales and movies. It's not how life works.

"So, you think Janie is reformed?" I asked David, aka Tonina. We had talked the day before school. I told him to stay in school and warned that teen marriages are usually doomed. Despite my advice, David dropped out, and they got married. The marriage resulted in a little girl named Providence, who died a year later. Janie's father had been against the union and tried to have it annulled. But it was too late. Both of them took it hard. A year later, Janie started drinking, and Lucas let himself go.

Over time, David became depressed and regained all his weight. The old Lucas had resurfaced. Surrounded by failure, his Janie was constantly high and drunk most of the time— Lucas took his own life by crashing his car into a semi-truck. Their story became a legend, a cautionary tale.

It was during our class reunion that Tonina's name came up.

I've never forgotten Lucas or the guys who taunted him. They are long gone—some died from drug overdoses and alcoholism, others faded into the dustbin of history. But Big Tonina still haunts the collective memory of the West Side, larger than La Llorona.

Now that's another story.

READER AND ADVISOR

*O*ne late October, I drove out to the southern outskirts of town with my aunt in tow. She asked my grandma for permission to lend me for a few hours so she could conduct business that required assistance, since she didn't drive. She discussed the details with Grandma, but I was not privy to them. Her husband, Nacho, had taken the delivery truck and wouldn't need the old Studebaker.

I was chosen as the chauffeur despite having no driver's license. I jumped at the chance because I loved driving their vehicle on small errands around the neighborhood. My aunt was tight-lipped about the trip. We drove out to the city's outskirts, passing businesses and gas stations for long stretches before I noticed the gas tank was half-full. I fidgeted with the radio but only got noise static. She informed me that it didn't work because of the receptor antennae. I sighed, oh well, and drove on. She basked in the serenity of the ride, taking in the dry scenery and the appeal of sacred silence. I often wondered why she didn't become a nun.

How far are we going, Aunty?"

"I'll tell you. Just keep driving," she said curtly.

That was my aunt in proper form, a woman of few words who barely added more syllables about any subject without bordering on conjecture and premature exaggeration. My aunt was private about her affairs. I glanced at the fuel gauge.

"We need to gas up."

She said that a Shamrock gas station was over the hill. And then an old mom-and-pop grocery, Shamrock's Last Fill-Up sign, popped up on the right.

While I gassed up the vehicle, my aunt bought snacks and drinks. We continued driving on Interstate 35 toward a cluster of double-wide trailers and a few farms, set amidst miles of stark emptiness with dustier roads and fewer gas stations.

"Be careful with radar," she said.

Just like that, sure enough, a road sign with *Welcome to Pleasanton* popped up, and behind the billboard was a Texas DPS motorcycle patrolman hidden with radar, waiting for speeders and out-of-state plates to give them a hearty Texas welcome.

Twilight was descending.

I asked my aunt how much longer it would be. She was busy reading an improvised map on her lap. I flipped on the high beams to scan the hilly landscape of withered trees and brown autumn foliage. Looking in the rearview mirror, I could see fewer county road lights as we headed out of San Antonio. Aunt Bartola adjusted her reading glasses and took a flashlight to read her scribbled map. She studied it carefully; I edged closer to her with one eye on her map and the other on the road.

She caught me glancing at her map.

"Keep your eyes on the road. I want to get there in one piece."

And then, without warning, she shouted, "Turn right. Here."

I turned quickly, causing her to drop the flashlight and apply the brakes to adjust the vehicle's momentum. The Studebaker swerved to rebalance itself against the dirt road, causing a cloud

of dust. The car slid to a complete stop until the dust settled. I
saw the highway lead into an isolated trailer home community.

"Jesus! We could have gotten killed!"

"Come on, Aunty. You told me at the last minute."

She remained pensive and then pointed to a battered sign. It
was dark. She beamed her flashlight on the marker and then
flashed the light on her lap, studying the yellow, hand-drawn
map with a red X marking their destination. She smiled, and the
light again fell on a road sign.

"See, look!"

"What am I looking for? The sign doesn't say anything."

Aunty, who had terrible night vision, replied: "It says Canton
Road."

I did a double-take and saw nothing resembling what her
map indicated.

"There's nothing. It's barely readable. It reads Cant—Rd.—
not Canton Road. The missing letters are two bullet holes." But
she was stubborn as a mule, and nothing could convince her
otherwise. I restarted the Studebaker and continued driving.

"Turn where you see a white fence with a herd of goats," she
said.

"They all have herds of goats," I said.

I regretted doing Grandma a favor, but Aunt Bartola was her
favorite.

When I asked my aunt where and why? I was told it was
none of my business.

"You're the driver. Don't ask questions."

Aunt Bartola, who was the pushy one in the family, had been
my caretaker since the time my grandma ended up in the
county hospital for a whole month. The two-tone Studebaker
made a squeaky sound as it traveled down crunchy gravel roads.
We crossed a few tattered trailers until we turned into a long,
circular driveway with a canopy of oak trees hiding a double-
wide.

Turning into the crunchy driveway, the headlights beamed across the property, hitting a posted sign that read, "Reader and Advisor."

Then I knew what it was all about. For years, she wanted to get her fortune read. She had heard about this fortune teller through a friend, who said she was the best in the business. Her name was *Doña* Marrequita. She was good at forecasting the future with a deck of cards. Aunt Bartola was desperate because she was on her third husband, and things were going downhill. Bad luck followed her like bears on molasses.

"This is way out here in nowhere land," I said.

She kept quiet. Then I said, "I'll wait out here."

Suddenly, she scowled and added, "Nah. You're coming with me." She grabbed her handbag. I figured she was afraid. A woman of my dear aunt's age had no business traveling to the county's outskirts. I knew she was scared, but did not want to betray her feelings. She was a strong-willed woman, just like my grandmother. When we exited the vehicle, the night creatures echoed in the darkness, and a pungent stench of a dead skunk tainted the air. Crickets and night owls were like a singular chorus. I wanted to return to the Studebaker when I uttered: "Okay, Aunty. A good five dollars would influence me."

She stopped dead in her tracks and flipped open her handbag.

"There's a dollar. Remember who cleaned your butt when you were little. Let's go."

I replied: "Okay. You lead, I'll follow."

We fumbled through the darkness, going straight to a dim lightbulb with swirling moths. We got to the door and pressed the buzzer, followed by an automatic click. We entered and pushed a bell that was ding-donging, alerting the owners. It clicked, and we entered. The inside was painted a bland, hospital beige. There is no furniture except a long bench, a vending machine, and a vase with plastic flowers. It looked like a waiting room.

A woman came out from a side door and greeted us, "Marrequita will see you shortly. Please sit. Sodas and chips are a dollar each."

"Thanks, but no thanks," Aunt Barty said.

My stomach growled. We waited and waited, and then I spotted a brown mouse scurrying about and entered a tiny hole near the floorboard. I don't think my aunt saw it; otherwise, she would have screamed bloody murder.

A woman in a house dress came out minutes later and said, "She's ready for both of you."

I didn't want to intrude on her affairs, so I said, "I'll wait out here, *Tia*."

Aunt Bartola glared at me like I had spilled red Kool-Aid on her velvet sofa. She probably wanted me to be there as a bodyguard or for support. I got up and went with her. An old lady greeted us and touched our faces with knotty hands, which I thought was odd. She had porcelain skin, dark eyes, and a map of wrinkles on her face. She even looked like those old-time gypsies I remember seeing on Saturday Matinees with scary shows, such as *The Werewolf* with Lon Chaney. She also wore a long black skirt with a smokey, incensed shawl and ringed gold chandelier earrings. She had a headscarf with beady, piercing eyes. A scent of roses and lavender oil permeated the air. I was looking for a crystal ball to complete her description of my idea of fortune-tellers, but there was none.

She asked us to sit at a white linen table with a deck of Tarot cards in the middle. She sat in front of us. She asked Aunty to cut the cards. When she did that, the old woman laid them out and reshuffled the cards, opening the deck. She placed the cards on the table and told my aunt to cut them whenever possible. My aunt lifted the deck and divided it into two stacks. The old woman collected the cards and then reshuffled and flapped the deck sideways, revealing strange figurines of goofy characters and weird personages. Then she stacked them in three rows facing us. I was paying close attention to see if she had hidden any cards in her sleeves. I had seen magicians do tricks with cards during Carnival week.

"The first row represents the present, the second represents your past, and the last represents your future. Each row costs $7. If you want them all read, it's $15."

My aunt eyed the cards carefully and then opened her purse. She placed a $20 bill on the table. The old lady returned a $5 bill from under her sleeve. I watched, amazed at the skill of her actions. She was moving very fast.

"Let's begin," the old lady said.

The cards all looked extraordinary, and she began interpreting their meanings. The Empress favored Aunty, with Judgment next, followed by Lovers, Hangman, and the Fool. The cards revealed a nasty predisposition about my aunt. The old woman told her that she was suspicious of men because many had cheated on her. My aunt's eyes widened.

"Go on, you have my attention," my aunt said.

"You are married. All your former husbands have cheated on you. You've lost time and money." I wanted to tell Aunt Bartola that these swindlers usually tell people this.

Tears were streaming down my aunt's face. It gets worse. She told Aunt Bartola about her lost son, the dissolution of her estate, and her long-gone beloved Fifi, a rat-looking Chihuahua. I was astonished at *Doña* Marriquita's abilities. Then, the final session involved her future.

The old woman stared at the cards attentively.

"Beware of Friday the 13th. Do not go anywhere. Stay put at home. Follow your routine. Do not leave the house. Your husband will want to go to a party. That party is where you will meet your fate. Avoid it at all costs."

"What will happen if I go with him?"

The old woman looked at her and said, "Your fate will be sealed. You will lose him."

"But if he goes alone?"

"You will lose nothing."

The session ended. Aunt Bartola thanked her and slipped her a $5 bill as a tip. I stared in disbelief. She knew everything about poor Aunt Bartola. But how was this possible? Miracles, magic, and soothsayers were for suckers, and yet *Doña* Marriquita was intriguing and exciting.

On our drive back, my aunt was eerily silent. I wanted to get home as quickly as possible because I was tired. Aunt Bartola turned to me and said, "All this remains private. You are not to tell anyone about this—understand."

"I understand, *Tia.*"

We got home late, and I went straight to my room and hit the sack. The next day, Grandma asked me if everything was all right. I knew she was lying about what happened. I kept my promise and said, "Nothing much." She knew I was tight-lipped. I gulped down breakfast and went outside when I saw Aunt Bartola walking down the street. She and Nacho lived two blocks away, and I was surprised she was walking because Nacho always dropped her off before heading for work.

"Everything okay, *Tia?*"

"No."

"Oh, sorry."

"Don't be. You want to make some money?"

It could be wrong, but money was the influencer, and I needed it for my Dolby stereo.

"So, what's on your mind?"

She wanted me to get my field binoculars, drive her to Cortez Foods, wait across the highway, and observe the parking lot. Nacho worked at Cortez Foods Inc.

"For how long?"

"As long as it takes. I'm going to catch them in the act. I

know Nacho leaves the premises with a woman. They probably go to that secluded park at the corner."

"What are you planning on doing, *Tia*?" I didn't want to be an accessory to anything, but twenty dollars was tempting. So, we embarked on our long detective charade of spying on poor Nacho that evening. We dropped off Nacho at the processing plant, where he assembled microwave dinner platters. The company sold thousands of tamale dinners, enchilada plates, and microwavable fajita platters. Nacho was a supervisor at the plant, where many single women worked. He was a soft-spoken individual with a pleasant demeanor and a gentle approach to life. Aunt Bartola had met him at a dinner party hosted by one of her friends from City Hall. Bartola was retired, and Nacho was ten years her junior. She was attracted to youthful men. Nacho had been coming home late, and when Bartola asked why, he always said production schedules demanded overtime.

For three evenings straight, we parked across from Cortez Foods with my binoculars trained on the employee parking lot. Each night, Nacho emerged from the building at exactly 10:47 PM, walked to his truck, and drove straight home. No mysterious woman. No detours to secluded parks. Nothing but a tired man heading home after a long shift.

"Maybe they meet somewhere else," Aunt Bartola muttered on the third night, adjusting her position in the passenger seat.

"*Tia*, maybe there's no 'they' at all," I suggested, but she shot me a look that could freeze hell over.

The following Monday, I was surprised to see Aunt Bartola at Grandma's kitchen table, looking more haggard than usual. Her eyes were puffy, and she clutched a tissue in her weathered hands.

"What's wrong, *mija*?" Grandma asked, pouring coffee.

"It's Nacho," she said, her voice barely above a whisper. "He's been acting strange. Secretive. And there's this party Friday night—his company's annual Halloween party. He keeps insisting I come with him, but…" She looked up at me, remembering Dona Marriquita's warning. "I can't go. I just can't."

Grandma raised an eyebrow. "Since when do you turn down a party?"

Friday the 13th arrived gray and drizzling. Aunt Bartola stayed home, claiming a headache, while Nacho went to the company party alone. She called me three times that evening, each call more frantic than the last.

"What if something happens to him?" she asked during the third call.

"Nothing's going to happen, *Tia*. He's just at a work party."

But around midnight, her phone rang. I heard her gasp from two blocks away.

The next morning, I found Aunt Bartola on Grandma's porch, staring at nothing. Her face was pale, her hands trembling slightly.

"*Tia?* What happened?"

She looked at me with hollow eyes. "Nacho came home from the party with news. The plant is closing. Moving operations to Mexico. He's losing his job after fifteen years."

She added that Nacho was going to follow the operations to Mexico but decided against it because the owner wanted reassurances then and there, and Nacho was not about to agree without his wife's approval and presence. He knew she would have been opposed to that idea, and he informed the company bosses that he wouldn't be going to Mexico without his wife. She paused, wiping her nose with the tissue. "If I had gone with him to that party, I would have had to pretend to be supportive, help him network, and put on a brave face. Instead, she managed a weak smile. "Instead, I was here, safe, while he dealt with it alone. When he told me all about it, I thanked God I didn't go because I would never have agreed to return to Piedras Negras."

I sat down beside her. "So, you didn't lose him?"

"No, *mijo*. But I almost lost myself in my suspicions and fear." She folded the tissue carefully. "That fortune teller, she was right about Friday the 13th. My fate would have been sealed at that party—sealed as the bitter, suspicious woman I was becoming. By staying home, I saved myself from that."

She stood up slowly, straightening her dress. "Nacho and I, we're going to be fine. We'll figure out the job situation. But first, I owe him an apology for all that spying nonsense."

As she walked down the street toward her house, I realized that sometimes the most powerful fortune-telling isn't about predicting the future—it's about helping people recognize the present they're creating for themselves. *Doña* Marriquita hadn't saved Aunt Bartola from losing Nacho; she'd saved her from losing herself.

I never did get that Dolby stereo, but watching my aunt rediscover trust was worth more than any twenty-dollar bill.

PROMISES TO KEEP

*I*t's springtime. The redbud trees are blossoming, and the air is pregnant with the sweet scent of honeysuckle and jasmine. From the open window, the boy could smell the morning aroma of damp earth mingling with the scent of Mrs. Gutierrez's piping hot speckled-brown tortillas. Saturday meant playing baseball at the park, exploring Alazan Creek for arrowheads, and riding the bus downtown with the boys from the block.

But that was not to be, as Tomás was recovering from a stomach virus, sitting in his bedroom and reading Robert Frost —not because he enjoyed poetry, but because Sister Sophia had penciled his name on an assignment ledger when he was absent. Every student in class had chosen a poet to study, and so he had been assigned the New England poet. He looked wistfully at the lines he had copied from the book: "The woods are lovely, dark and deep, but I have promises to keep/And miles to go before I sleep...."

He was wondering how he could commit the lines to heart when he heard the phone ring.

After hearing his mother shuffle to the phone stand, "Tomás, it's for you," his mother said. "Remember, finish your home-work first, and then you can go out and play with Pedro."

Tomás had been thinking about Pedro, his friend, wondering if he would be going to Mexico for the Easter holidays. They attended Our Lady of Guadalupe Elementary School.

"Hello Pete, what's up?"

"Tom! You're not gonna believe this, but—" Pedro hesitated, wondering how to tell him delicately. "Old Man Garcia is on his knees and crawling down the street."

"Slow down. What? Who?"

"Old Man Garcia. He's on his knees," Pedro said.

"On his knees? Why? Where is he going?"

"Ah, come on, you know. Well, ah...." Pedro said impatiently. "He's probably heading to the church. He's made a promesa," he added, leaving the word hanging palpably in Tomás's ear.

"A promesa, heh?" Tomás said.

The word left a sour taste in his mouth. Tomás disapproved of promesas because he thought them futile.

"So, where exactly is he?" Tomás asked.

"Well, the way I figure it, he should be crawling past your house in about five minutes. I'll be over in a jiffy. Okay?"

Pedro hung up the receiver before Tomás could tell him he didn't want any part of it because the penitents brought out the worst in people. He looked out the window and saw a group of neighbors trudging down the hill like snails, a procession inching its way through the barrio. At the center was the peni-tent, moving along awkwardly. Now and then, when the people moved aside, Tomás could see him in the briefly opening gaps, crawling painfully on his knees as he passed beneath the towering image of a cross-shaped telephone pole. His scuffed shoes and raggy, baggy pants had a humility about them, for the penitent was an ordinary man, a familiar man with a pale, unas-suming face and dark, sad eyes.

It was an all-too-familiar ritual. Every year during Lent, the penitents made their obligatory pilgrimages, drawing the faithful to neighborhood churches. Tomás thought it all useless because after the ritual, the penitents returned to their sinful ways—promises unfulfilled—and everything felt in vain. In his heart, Tomás believed that life, like the seasons, was one continuous, repeating cycle. His life and that of the penitent were eternal, like the expanding cosmos—a nightmare without end until heaven, as Sister Sophia incessantly reminded them, opened its gates to receive all sinners.

Perhaps the Sisters of Guadalupe had provided fertile ground for his imagination because they taught repentance through suffering, or possibly Tomás had acquired his doubts from the Greek books he had checked out from the public library, which suggested that suffering is the key to knowledge. Even so, at Guadalupe, Tomás learned about the purity of the soul, the beauty of heaven, and the fires of hell. He knew how Jesus had survived forty days and forty nights in the desert, and how the Son of God had shunned temptation. Only the Son of God could do this, Tomás reasoned, because He is not of this world. The penitent was just a man with human blood flowing through his arteries, bearing human imperfection in his soul, a man living in a world full of Miracle, Mystery, and Authority. Only God could endure forty days and forty nights in the desert. It was far too much to ask of anyone, Tomás thought, because they were only human, after all.

Such questions had long tortured Tomás since he could remember. Seeing the penitent only made it worse. Tomás knew the penitents could not change because he had seen others fail to alter their lives. He wondered: Why did God demand sacrifice from lesser beings than He? The boy had asked the stern-faced Father Jonas this blasphemous question ("If God knows everything, doesn't He know people are going to repeat sins?" Father Jonas, muttering, "God sees all, knows all, forgives all.")

It wasn't enough, for Tomás felt the weight of his knowledge. He turned his gaze back to the penitent, questioning why he even attempted such sacrifices. Was he imitating Christ? He shook his head, trying to clear his feelings about the old man, and thought about his father, who had made a thousand similar promises to porcelain saints, swearing he would never do this or that, never touch a whiskey bottle; in the end, everything would fall apart because his father would resume drinking until another year passed and another promesa to stay away from the cantinas. Why couldn't his father admit that he was a sinner, addicted to alcohol? Maybe then, with understanding, he could have saved himself.

"Tomás! Tomás!"

His mother's voice awoke him from his reverie.

"Are you daydreaming again, Tomás?"

"No, Mama."

"Have you finished your homework?"

"Yes, Mama."

His mother worked five days a week, nearly fifteen hours a day, to give him a decent Catholic education. She worried that he spent too much time thinking about his deceased father and asking too many questions for a little boy who couldn't understand.

"Pedro is here to see you," she said.

Pedro stood at the doorway.

A tiny waif, a foot shorter than Tomás, with doe-like eyes, seemed more accepting than curious, and had a soft, almost whispering voice that other boys thought was meekness. Pedro believed in the incarnation of the spirit, in the Word as Sister Sophia taught, and in the four archangels who guard the four corners of the earth. He was the boy who earned the highest grade in religion class and believed that all life has a purpose in the ordered universe. As an acolyte for Sunday service, Pedro went to great lengths to serve the Host with such ritual precision and solemnity that even Father Jonas, with admiration in his eyes, said Pedro was probably destined to become a priest.

Pedro and Tomás saw the world through different lenses. One believed in the incorporeal nature of the heavens, in absolute faith and the subjugation of pride; the other had become captivated by the intellect and the human soul with all its flaws. They had a precocity uncommon for their age. Even their questions had a philosophical fervor. ("Do all creatures go to heaven?" Tomás asked Pedro. "Yes, even the meek shall enter the Kingdom of God," Pedro would reply. "And if a mouse eats the Host, does God enter its body?" With a sheepish grin, Pedro would retort, "That is for God to decide, not me.") It was their differences that brought them together, each trying desperately to convince the other that his way of seeing things was the true reality behind the shadow.

One could say that Tomás had his feet firmly on the ground, listening to the soft tremors of Mother Earth while Pedro, his watchful eye, like the stone sentinels of Easter Island, gazed vigilantly at the heavens. Tomás questioned the world with the skepticism of a scientist, breaking down the microcosm of the infinitesimal while Pedro, the inveterate stargazer, sought the celestial lifeblood that united God and humanity, and the innate goodness of people as they struggled toward perfection.

"Would you care for some milk with pan dulce, Pedro?" Tomás's mother asked.

He bit his lip and said, "*No gracias.*"

She left and closed the door.

"Well, what are we waiting for?" Pedro asked. "Let's go. You think he'll make it?"

He sensed that Tomás was not in his usual mood but driven by a desperate desire to prove God's benevolence, he urged Tomás to come. Perhaps this time, someone would succeed. And maybe this time, Father Jonas wouldn't intervene, would let the man fulfill his promise.

"Make it? Make what?" Tomás responded half-heartedly.

"You know—to the church."

"Uh, yeah, yeah. Sure, he'll make it there just fine."

"Please, Tom. Don't be like that."

Tomás looked at Pedro for a long time and smiled and said, "I'm sorry. Come on, let's go. But don't be disappointed."

OLD MAN GARCIA, as the neighborhood boys called him, was a carpenter. Desperate because medicine couldn't save his son, who was dying of cancer in a hospital bed, Emiliano Garcia decided to humbly seek help from his community, his family, and his God. The way Emiliano saw it, he was turning to God's infinite mercy and hoping that his cries, public and unabashed, would create a miracle.

It was an enormous five-mile journey, marked by four long blocks of intense pain over asphalt and concrete, scattered with pebbles and broken glass. As he moved slowly down Guadalupe Street on his knees, pressing against the hard pavement, his odyssey turned into a torment, with a swarm of the faithful clutching rosaries and praying the Hail Mary, full of grace, the Lord is with thee...; no one could deny that the penitent was in great pain. The closer he got, the more it seemed he still had to go. His sporadic groans were accompanied by the "Ave Marias" and "¡Ay Dios Míos!" every step of the way. His promesa had become their promesas; his groan became their groans, his goal their goals, until it was hard to tell who was truly on the journey.

But even the penitent was not immune to criticism. Some despised the penitents for their selfish reasons. However, it was the skeptics who wanted the penitent to fail, taunting him with "Nothing's gonna save you, old man! Who do you think you are, anyway, Jesus Christ?" Their failures cast a shadow over the old man.

Slowly, inch by inch toward his goal, Old Man Garcia felt his knees weakening, a numbness winding like a snake around his legs, nearly paralyzing them. But the penitent had a stubborn zeal. They won't give up, he thought; they want me to fail. I will not fail. Little Emilio will live, even if the doctors say no.

"Crawl, old man. Tell us your sins. Confess your sins!" Petra, his neighbor and the first to see him, barked from her fence. She despised him because he had unmasked himself before them; he had revealed his humility.

"It's all useless. You're wasting your life. Don't be stupid. Save yourself. That's the only thing that counts," she shouted.

Old Man Garcia was deaf to their taunting; his eyes gazed skyward, completely entranced, as he mumbled his prayers in a nearly chant-like manner. His thoughts centered on a suffering image of little Emilio on the white sheets of a hospital bed, tubes connected to his arms, a phosphorescent monitor beeping and tracing lines that Garcia dreaded. Emilio, *por Dios*, don't die. Please don't die, my son. You have given so much of yourself to us; now it is time for your father to give unto you.

It had come as a shock to Old Man Garcia when little Emilio announced one day that he wanted to become a priest. A black bile rose from the pit of his gut, twisting and choking his sensibilities with a knowledge that his son would not follow the family business like his father before him.

Being a priest was something that happened to others, not him. The priesthood was a vocation separate from the path of life. It was something alien to him, and his loathing for what the priesthood symbolized had lain dormant within him since the days of the Cristero Rebellion in Zacatecas. Little Emiliano approached him and asked his father why he was so against it.

"I just don't want you to become a priest, that's all," the old man gruffly said.

"Why, Father? Is it because you won't have grandsons?"

The old man silently walked away.

"I'm sorry, Father, if I offended you," Emiliano said.

The old man was a million miles away, mute to his son's pleadings, resolved to work harder each day until his family and little Emiliano became a blur in his fading memory. I'm sorry, my son, if I have broken your heart, but I cannot let you sacrifice your life. It is I who needs to be forgiven, not you.

When the penitent discovered his son was dying of cancer, a heavy veil of guilt pressed against his chest like a boulder; indeed, his legs became as solid as granite, his limbs rock-hard until the unbearable weight of his conscience forced him to bend his knees and submit his pride to humility. But it was fear, more than guilt, that compelled him to journey toward the absolution of his sins. He wondered if Almighty Jehovah would forgive him for standing in the way of his son's vocation.

Pedro and Tomás arrive just in time to watch Old Man Garcia cross the boulevard, moving slowly and deliberately into the street leading directly to Our Lady of Guadalupe Church. The boys see people they have known for years taunting the old man.

"Look, there's Mrs. Gutierrez. She's always on time for ten o'clock mass," Pedro whispers, quite stunned. This deeply troubles Pedro, who, unlike Tomás, is unaware of the darker side of the people in the barrio. Throughout the neighborhood, people stand and watch. The women, gathered by the fence and clutching their babies, are careful not to miss the penitent; the men, awestruck and almost dumbfounded by the courage or stupidity of these deeds, wonder secretly if a time will come when they must perform such desperate acts.

And so, when the frail sixty-five-year-old carpenter decided to undertake the pilgrimage—a journey toward salvation—it became one horrific trial. Old Man Garcia discovered the dark side of his neighbors, most of whom encouraged him yet believed his act futile and his son doomed. They despised him because he had never set foot inside the church since his son's baptism. Was he a hypocrite? Nevertheless, the penitent felt that his journey would purge him of his pride and expiate the guilt he felt for his lack of fatherhood and the sins committed against his brethren.

But something nagged him. What if his son died even after this great sacrifice? Would he turn a deaf ear toward God? Tomás pondered this question as he stared at the penitent, who already knew the answer. Just as Tomás was about to touch the old man's shoulder, Petra Gonzalez, his neighbor, shouted: "Whatever it is you've done, you can't wash it off with this feat. You'll lose your self-respect when you find out nothing changes. Accept what you cannot change, old man!"

Pedro watched Petra approach the penitent; he noticed her eyes fixated on Garcia's pain. Then her whole body seemed to tremble as she broke down in tears. It was as if a cross had been lifted from her shoulders. Petra realized she had been resenting the penitent because of his strength and endurance in withstanding the vicissitudes of life.

"See how God works," Pedro said.

"Yes, now both are in misery," Tomás retorted.

"But look at Petra. She's changed."

"For how long?"

And yet, Tomás could not deny the change in her face; he could not understand the strange calmness that surrounded her. The woman suddenly dropped to her knees and prayed, and Tomás, still observing, was overwhelmed by the unusual connection between Petra and Pedro. He watched as the penitent continued his journey.

At the traffic light, the honking cars and the disgruntled pedestrians came to a sudden halt as the penitent crossed the intersection and came closer to his goal. And then, unexpectedly, Old Man Garcia shifted his eyes from the heavens and stared directly at Tomás. Something about the penitent looked strangely different. Tomás felt it immediately when he stared into his dark eyes—a feeling of peace rested in those eyes as if the old man felt no pain but floated like a cloud. And then, almost mysteriously, Pedro, understanding the effect of the penitent, saw pity and sorrow in Tomás's eyes and felt empathy for him. He had seen those pictures of Jesus nailed to the cross, and now Tomás seemed to have those same eyes. Was the miracle of faith beginning to descend on Tomás?

"Look, he bleeds," Pedro whispered. Tomás turned, silently staring at his friend. He remembered how Pedro's father had died, a working man entirely devoted to responsibility. Sacrifice, Pedro's father taught, was the path to righteousness. Pedro was never ashamed to admit mistakes or to submit his pride to humility. When Pedro found out a drunk driver had killed his father, Tomás never forgot how Pedro, after struggling for months with his father's death, confronted the guilty person in court and told him he didn't hate him. Taken aback, the man, biting his lip, begged the boy's forgiveness.

"He's gotta stop. Don't you see, he'll die," Tomás pleaded.

This cry seemed to energize the crowd even more. The penitent was crawling closer to Our Lady of Guadalupe Church; it was only a few minutes before the ordeal would come to an end. The parish priest had already come halfway to meet him.

"Look, it's Father Jonas," Pedro sighed.

"Good," Tomás said, hoping that the penitent would at least get a respite.

"I hope he continues," Pedro said.

"What for?"

"The promesa."

The crowd parted for Father Jonas. "*Con permiso por favor. Please let me through, please,*" Father Jonas pleaded in Spanish. The penitent scraped his knees with more momentum as he hurried on his journey, inch by inch, his knees moving in jerky tension, right then left, right then left.

Father Jonas was accustomed to seeing penitents. He had

encountered so many that he often doubted their sincerity. In short, he saw them as spectacles meant for carnivals, not for solemn acts during Lent. Father Jonas usually suppressed his doubts and reservations through prayer and meditation. Sometimes, his actions betrayed his true feelings. Unlike his fellow priests, Father Jonas would show a slight revulsion—a cold sneer here, a twitch of the lip there, a condescending brow, sometimes even a mechanical pace during mass, as if serving with a troubled soul.

"*Señor* Garcia, please. You can stop now. This penance is hurting you more than helping. Christ would disapprove of us making such harsh promises. Christ doesn't require sacrifices, but love. We must love one another; that is the greatest sacrifice Christ makes," Father Jonas pleaded.

"Is this, not love?" the penitent groaned, breaking his silence.

Father Jonas stared at the sea of faces: skeptics who grinned and waited to see when the penitent would stand and admit failure; the faithful who watched, murmuring their incantations, clutching their rosaries, seeking guidance from Father Jonas's wisdom. He had spoken with the penitent only a month earlier when Old Man Garcia had come to the rectory to make a special offering; he wanted a particular mass for his son.

As Father Jonas stared at the faithful, a quivering sensation seized his right eye; frightened, he felt his soul slipping beneath him. Oh, Heavenly Father, help me guide these people on the right path; I'm weak and dispirited, and sometimes I feel that I'm being punished as well. Bring clarity to this poor man. Guide the faithless, anoint the wretched, and save the wicked. Save me, oh Lord. Please save me. Give me the words to respond to this man.

"He won't listen to you, Father," Tomás said, staring at the glassy-eyed penitent.

"Huh? What's that?" Father Jonas was jolted.

"I mean, he's out of it. Just look at him. He's not listening. He's just crawling toward his destination."

"You mean, destiny," Pedro corrected him.

"No, destination."

Father Jonas flushed; his cobalt blue eyes stabbing the stoic Tomás. He never knew what to expect from that boy.

The penitent was closer to the steps of Our Lady of Guadalupe Church. The skeptics, disgruntled by his apparent victory, were losing interest, while the faithful, their hearts uplifted, were chanting "Hallelujah, Hallelujah" louder. He had crossed the courtyard before the church.

The church stood before him, its steeple reaching into the blue sky. The church bells rang out. The priest crept beside the penitent, almost pensive as he counted each step, imagining how Christ might have felt during each station of the cross.

Old Man Garcia arched his back and looked up at the sky. Suddenly, the crowd was hit by a strong gust of wind, dust, and grit that temporarily blinded everyone. The penitent paused, catching his breath, and gazed at Tomás, sensing tragedy in his eyes and a feeling of impending doom. He saw the image of his son on the hospital bed. (Will someone inform the nearest relative that Emilio Garcia has passed away.) Like a powerful shuddering thought stabbing his bones, Old Man Garcia began trembling, tears streaming down his face, an inexplicable sadness filling his body, followed by a sense of unfathomable loss, a feeling of detachment from the outside world. When the penitent stopped, Pedro said,

"You can't stop, Mr. Garcia; it's only inches away now."

Father Jonas asked the old man if he wanted to stand while a woman from across the street brought him a wheelchair. There was pity in the eyes of the faithful, but scorn in the eyes of the skeptics who remained. With outstretched arms, Father Jonas offered to support him, but the old man's tenacity was unshakable. First the right leg, then the left leg, as the penitent inched his way to the periphery of the church grounds.

"Look! Tom. A promesa is almost complete," Pedro said.

"And if the penitent dies?" Tomás asked. But Tomás felt deeply for the old man, and Pedro could almost sense his friend's sadness, as if he deeply felt the wound of his mortality.

Pedro had taken an interest in the penitent not because he had seen many who claimed repentance, but because the old man reflected honesty and piety in his unselfish act. He wanted so much for the old man to complete his promesa because Pedro believed that suffering would not go unrewarded by the Holy Heavens. For Pedro, life was part of the greater cosmos, breathing life and demanding death, as the forces of nature existed in harmony with the living earth. Tomás, however, believed that God was alone in the universe, and humankind was alone on earth. And what did this penitent have to do with them? Tomás had warned him that putting too much faith in the success of the penitent would only lead to disappointment if Old Man Garcia failed in his promesa.

The penitent scanned the audience. Could the old man see into their hearts, Tomás wondered. Suddenly, Tomás felt his heartbeat quicken; his forehead became moist, and his inner sky darkened, with lightning flashing. Just as the penitent reached the last step leading to the door, he collapsed.

The faithful gasped, "¡Dios mío! Help him, Father. Father Jonas, help him."

Pedro and Tomás hurried to help the priest support the old man, but the penitent was too weak. Tomás could feel Old Man Garcia's defeated limbs as Pedro, urging him to lie the man down, saw his bloodied pants. The old man gasped for air, collapsing again, as Father Jonas placed his ear against the old man's chest.

"Come on, don't die on me now, for heaven's sake," Father Jonas uttered. The priest began pounding frantically on his chest, rhythmically, again and again. "Please, don't let him die. Oh Lord," he prayed. "Please, don't let him die." But the old man was slipping away. "This man cannot die, Lord!"

With no time to spare, Father Jonas lifted the old man and carried him into the church. If the penitent couldn't make it inside, Father Jonas made sure the old man would enter the sanctuary before his last breath. Women dressed in black prayed steadily and mournfully, understanding that the old man was passing away. Tomás and Pedro stared solemnly at each other, fully aware that the old man wouldn't survive. Tomás felt sorry for the penitent because he had secretly wished for his failure. Maybe, Tomás thought, it was because God had never answered his promesa when his father was dying. Tomás wanted so badly to believe in miracles—oh, yes, how much he longed to believe in them.

It was so unfair, Tomás thought, that God only answered a few prayers, if at all. Watching the penitent, Father Jonas realized it was pointless because his vacant eyes were quickly dimming. Still, Father Jonas did not give up.

The procession followed the priest carrying the penitent in his arms into the altar amid a chorus of *Dios mío...Santo Jesús...* and a litany of prayers, all aimed at bringing salvation to the wretched man's soul.

Inside the lavish church with its fourteen stained glass windows, each depicting the stations of the cross, Father Jonas sat, gazing at the old man who had completed his promesa. It was ironic, Tomás thought, that the penitent had died inside the church next to a statue of the crucified Christ, who peered down at him as if man and God were both meant to suffer and endure forever: the penitent's eyes, without gleam, faced the humble features of the crucified Christ, as if a union had occurred—maybe even a miracle.

It was not until Easter Sunday that Tomás and Pedro discovered what had happened to little Emilio.

After mass, Pedro asked Tomás, "What was that word Father Jonas used about Emilio's condition?"

"Oh, twilight sleep. What about it?"

"Well, what does it mean to you?"

Tomás looked at Pedro for a long moment and said, "It means Old Man Garcia won't get his wish. His son has fallen into a coma. He's as good as dead."

"Ohh," Pedro said.

There was a long gulf of silence.

"Maybe next year," Tomás said, as he put his arm around Pedro's shoulder.

ACKNOWLEDGMENTS

This book was written with the help of numerous colleagues and friends who have provided me with encouragement and intellectual sustenance through their guidance, unwavering support, and friendship. I am grateful to Belinda Urdiales, my partner and editor, who questioned every twist and turn of my plots and character development. Whenever I fumbled, she was there to ensure my ego wasn't hurt. I would also like to thank Julian S. Garcia, a longtime friend from my elementary school years, for his unwavering support and for reading much of the material in this book. A writer, scholar, and editor himself, Julian has interesting stories and an abundance of patience and provided the introduction.

A special thanks for editorial support to Josh Brodesky, Arthur Carvajal, Melissa Murphy, Misty Harris, O. Pimentel, Robert Seltzer, Maria Martha Brummel, Caroline Mains, Diane Lerma, Antonio Villanueva, Lennie Irvin, Vicente Guillot, Daniel Rodriguez, David O. Martinez, Daniel Hernandez, Ignacio Garcia, Sabina Cerda, Teresa Gonzalez, Maria Aurora Yanez, Cecilia Sublette, Jenny Scheidt, Chris "Rooster" Martinez, Jennifer Andermatt, and the entire English Department at Palo Alto College.

Literary and scholarly supporters include Vincent Bosquez, Fernando E. Flores, Don Graham, Steven G. Kellman, Robert Seltzer, Rogelio Saenz, Alfredo Torres Jr., and Tino Villanueva.

Special thanks to Little, Brown, & Company editor Kurt

Wilson; George and Andrea Velasquez, editors; and Philip Dunshea, Editor at Peter Lang International.

To the excellent staff at *Tiltwood Press*, copy readers Katrina Starasinic, Marizel Urdiales, Raquel Urdiales, and Janel Urdiales (Art Director); writers, artists, and poets of *Voces Cosmicas*, with special thanks to Jacinto Jesus Cardona, Fernando Esteban Flores, Alex Salinas, Alicia Galvan, and Rita Ortiz.

A shoutout to literary influencers Mariano Azuela, Rudolfo Anaya, Ray Bradbury, James Baldwin, John Cheever, E.L. Doctorow, Fyodor Dostoevsky, Annie Ernaux, William Faulkner, Gustave Flaubert, Franz Kafka, Mark Helprin, F. Scott Fitzgerald, Juan Rulfo, Norman Mailer, Gabriel Garcia Marquez, Toni Morrison, Vladimir Nabokov, Susan Sontag, Americo Paredes, Tino Villanueva, Virginia Woolf, and Malcolm X.

The following stories "Marfa Lights," "The Language of Sparrows," and "The Last Time" appeared in different form in the *College Humanities Review* (Spring/Fall 2021; Fall/Spring 2023; Fall/Spring 2024) with special thanks to Sidney Elliot, editor-in-chief of the journal; to the editors (Natalia M. Toscano, Gustavo Garcia, Elizabeth Gonzales-Cardenas, Jose Luis Serrano Najera, and Irene Vasquez) of the inaugural journal *Regeneración* published at the University of New Mexico where "Lucas AKA Tonina" first appeared. The story, "Promises to Keep," appeared in a different format in *New Growth/2: Contemporary Short Stories by Texas Writers*, edited by Mark Busby. "A Winter's Tale" appeared in a different format in *Aurora* (Floricanto Press), 2010.

ABOUT THE AUTHOR

Rafael C. Castillo teaches literature and humanities at Palo Alto College. He is an editor with *Catch the Next, Inc.* (New Haven, CT) and is the author of *Distant Journeys, Aurora,* and *Dostoevsky on Guadalupe Street.* His fiction has been anthologized in *Lone Star Literature* (Norton), *Under the Promegranate Tree* (Washington Square Press), *Southwest Tales* (Colorado), and *New Growth II* (Corona Press).

ALSO BY RAFAEL C. CASTILLO

Distant Journeys (Bilingual Review Press/Arizona State University), 1991

Aurora (Floricanto Press), 2010

Dostoevsky on Guadalupe Street: Essays (Peter Lang International), 2023

www.ingramcontent.com/pod-product-compliance
Lightning Source LLC
Chambersburg PA
CBHW030516260626
47157CB00005B/1764